Praise for Ali Smith's

Winter

**Shortlisted for the British Book Award
Fiction Book of the Year and
the Orwell Prize for Political Writing**

"There are few writers on the world stage who are producing fiction this offbeat and alluring."
—*The New York Times*

"Breathtaking. . . . [Smith] is one of the rarest creatures in the world: a really fearless novelist."
—*Chicago Tribune*

"*Winter* is a stunning meditation on a complex, emotional moment in history. The outlook at the end is dark, but soon enough *Spring* will come, and then maybe the threatening icicles will thaw and the buds of hope will push through."
—*Time*

"Magnificent. . . . Stunningly original. . . . Ali Smith is writing a classic, one mind-blowing installment at a time."
—*Milwaukee Journal Sentinel*

"The second in Smith's quartet of seasonal novels displays her mastery at weaving allusive magic into the tragicomedies of British people and politics. . . . A bleak, beautiful tale." —*Vulture*

"Astonishingly fertile and free. . . . Dickensian in its fluency and mobile empathy. . . . [Smith] fashions a novel which, in its very inclusiveness, associative joy and unrestricted movement, proposes other kinds of vision. . . . Leaping, laughing, sad, generous and winterwise, this is a thing of grace." —*The Guardian*

"Luminously beautiful. . . . A novel of great ferocity, tenderness, righteous anger and generosity of spirit that you feel Dickens would have recognised. . . . There is forgiveness here, and song, and comic resolution of sorts, but the abiding image is of the tenacity of nature and light." —*The Observer* (London)

ali smith
Winter

Ali Smith was born in Inverness, Scotland, in 1962 and lives in Cambridge, England. She is the author of *Autumn*, *How to be both*, *There but for the*, *Artful*, *Free Love*, *Like*, *Hotel World*, *Other Stories and other stories*, *The Whole Story and other stories*, *The Accidental*, *Girl Meets Boy*, and *The First Person and other stories*. *Hotel World* and *The Accidental* were both shortlisted for the Man Booker Prize and the Orange Prize. *How to be both* won the Baileys Women's Prize for Fiction, the Goldsmiths Prize, and the Costa Book of the Year Award and was shortlisted for the Man Booker Prize. *Autumn* was shortlisted for the 2017 Man Booker Prize.

Winter

ali smith
Winter

A Novel

Anchor Books
A Division of Penguin Random House LLC
New York

FIRST ANCHOR BOOKS EDITION, NOVEMBER 2018

Copyright © 2017 by Ali Smith

All rights reserved. Published in the United States by Anchor Books,
a division of Penguin Random House LLC, New York. Originally
published in hardcover in Great Britain by Hamish Hamilton, an imprint
of Penguin Books Ltd., a division of Penguin Random House Ltd.,
London, in 2017, and subsequently published in hardcover in the United
States by Pantheon Books, a division of Penguin Random House LLC,
New York, in 2018.

The Library of Congress has cataloged the Pantheon edition as follows:
Name: Smith, Ali, [date] author.
Title: Winter / Ali Smith.
Description: First United States edition. New York : Pantheon Books,
    [2018]
Identifiers: LCCN 2017043695
Classification: LCC PR6069.M4213 W56 2018. DDC 823/.914—dc23
LC record available at https://lccn.loc.gov/2017043695

Anchor Books Trade Paperback ISBN: 978-1-101-96995-3
eBook ISBN: 978-1-101-87076-1

www.anchorbooks.com

Printed in the United States of America
10 9 8 7 6 5 4 3 2 1

For Sarah Daniel
in the lion's den
with love

and for Sarah Wood
muß i' denn
with love

Nor the furious winter's rages.
William Shakespeare

Landscape directs its own images.
Barbara Hepworth

But if you believe you're a citizen of the world,
you're a citizen of nowhere.
Theresa May, 5 October 2016

We have entered the realm of mythology.
Muriel Spark

Darkness is cheap.
Charles Dickens

1

God was dead: to begin with.

And romance was dead. Chivalry was dead. Poetry, the novel, painting, they were all dead, and art was dead. Theatre and cinema were both dead. Literature was dead. The book was dead. Modernism, postmodernism, realism and surrealism were all dead. Jazz was dead, pop music, disco, rap, classical music, dead. Culture was dead. Decency, society, family values were dead. The past was dead. History was dead. The welfare state was dead. Politics was dead. Democracy was dead. Communism, fascism, neoliberalism, capitalism, all dead, and marxism, dead, feminism, also dead. Political correctness, dead. Racism was dead. Religion was dead. Thought was dead. Hope was dead. Truth and fiction were both dead. The media was dead. The internet was dead. Twitter, instagram, facebook, google, dead.

Love was dead.

Death was dead.

A great many things were dead.

Some, though, weren't, or weren't dead yet.

Life wasn't yet dead. Revolution wasn't dead. Racial equality wasn't dead. Hatred wasn't dead.

But the computer? Dead. TV? Dead. Radio? Dead. Mobiles were dead. Batteries were dead. Marriages were dead, sex lives were dead, conversation was dead. Leaves were dead. Flowers were dead, dead in their water.

Imagine being haunted by the ghosts of all these dead things. Imagine being haunted by the ghost of a flower. No, imagine being haunted (if there were such a thing as being haunted, rather than just neurosis or psychosis) by the ghost (if there were such a thing as ghosts, rather than just imagination) of a flower.

Ghosts themselves weren't dead, not exactly. Instead, the following questions came up:

are ghosts dead
are ghosts dead or alive
are ghosts deadly

but in any case forget ghosts, put them out of your mind because this isn't a ghost story, though it's the dead of winter when it happens, a bright sunny post-millennial global-warming Christmas Eve morning (Christmas, too, dead), and it's about real things really happening in the real world involving real people in real time on the real earth (uh huh, earth, also dead):

Good morning, Sophia Cleves said. Happy
day-before-Christmas.

She was speaking to the disembodied head.

It was the head of a child, just a head, no body
attached, floating by itself in mid air.

It was tenacious, the head. This was its fourth
day in her house; she'd opened her eyes this
morning and it was still here, this time hovering
over the washbasin watching itself in the mirror. It
swivelled to face her as soon as she spoke to it and
when it saw her, it – can something with no neck or
shoulders be said to bow? it definitely dipped itself,
sort of tipped forward with its eyes down respectful
then up again courtly and bright, a bow, or a
curtsey? Was it male or female? What it was was
very well mannered, polite, the head of a good

polite child (still pre-language, maybe, because quite silent) now the size of a cantaloupe (was it ironic or a failing, to be more at home with melons than children? lucky for her, Arthur'd caught on quickly when he was small that she preferred children to aspire to being less childlike), though quite unlike a melon in that it had a face, and a thick head of hair a couple of inches longer than itself, straggly, rich, dark, wavy-straight, rather romantic like a miniature cavalier if it was male, or if female something like the child adorned in leaves in the park in Paris with her back to the camera on the old black and white postcard of the photograph taken by the twentieth century French photographer Édouard Boubat (*petite fille aux feuilles mortes jardin du Luxembourg Paris 1946*) and when Sophia'd first woken this morning and seen it there, the head with the back of its head to her, its hair had been doing the beguiling thing of lifting and falling slightly in the central-heating air, but only on the one side, the side directly above the radiator; now it swayed and wafted a fragment of a moment behind the head's free-floating shifts and balances like a slow-motion soft-focus person's hair does in a shampoo commercial. See? Shampoo commercial is not ghost or ghoul. Nothing scary about it.

(Unless shampoo commercials, or maybe all commercials, *are* actually frightful visions of the living dead and it's just that we've become so accustomed to them that we're no longer shocked.)

In any case, it just wasn't frightening, the head. It was sweet, and bashful in its ceremoniousness, and those aren't words you can associate with a dead thing or the notion of the marauding spirit of a dead thing – and it didn't seem in the least dead, though it looked like it might maybe be a little more grisly underneath at the place where a neck would once have been, where there was the rumour, just, of something more visceral, shredded, meaty.

But anything too much like that was tucked well behind the hair and the chin, not the first thing that struck you, which was the *life* in it, the warmth of its demeanour, and as it bobbed and nodded merrily in the air next to her like a little green buoy in untroubled water while Sophia washed her face and cleaned her teeth, and as it skimmed airily the descent ahead of Sophia down the stairs and wove itself, little planet in its own micro-universe, in and out between the dusty twigs of the collection of dead orchids on the lower landing, it radiated more benignity than the head of any Buddha that Sophia'd yet encountered, painted head of any Cupid or stupefied Christmas cherubim.

In the kitchen Sophia put water and coffee in the espresso maker. She screwed the top part of the espresso maker on and lit the gas. As she did the head veered away from the sudden heat. Its eyes were full of laughter. As if for fun it dared itself towards and away from the flame.

You'll catch your hair on fire, she said.

The head shook its head. She laughed. Delightful.

I wonder if it knows what Christmas is, if it knows about Christmas Eve.

What child doesn't?

I wonder what the trains are like today. I wonder if it'd like me to take it to London. We could go to Hamleys. The Christmas lights.

We could go to the zoo. I wonder if it's ever been to the zoo. Children love the zoo. I wonder if the zoo's open this close to Christmas. Or we could go and see, I don't know, guardsmen, they'll be there regardless of Christmas with the bearskins on, the red tunics. That'd be something splendid. Or the Science Museum, where you can see things like your own bones through your hands.

(Ah.

The head didn't have any hands.)

Well, I could push the buttons *for* it, the interactive things, I could do those things for it if it can't do them for itself. Or the V and A. Things of such beauty, no matter how old or young you are. The Natural History Museum. I can tuck it inside my coat. I'll take a big bag. I'll cut eyeholes. I'll fold a scarf for the bottom of the bag, a jumper, something soft.

The head was on the windowsill sniffing at what was left of the supermarket thyme. It closed its eyes in what looked like pleasure. It rubbed its forehead against the tiny leaves. The scent of thyme spread through the kitchen and the plant toppled into the sink.

While it was in there, the plant, Sophia turned on the tap and gave it a drink.

Then she sat at the table with the coffee. The head settled next to the fruitbowl, apples, lemons. It made her table look like an art joke, an installation or a painting by the artist Magritte, This Isn't a Head; no, like Dalí, or the De Chirico heads, but funny, like Duchamp who put the moustache on the Mona Lisa, even something like a tabletop still life by Cézanne whom she'd always found on the one hand unsettling and on the other refreshing given that he reveals, though it's hard to believe, that things like apples and oranges can be blues and purples as well, colours you would never have believed they had in them.

In one of the papers recently she'd seen a picture of what looked like a wall of people standing in front of the wall on which the Mona Lisa hangs in the Louvre. She'd seen, herself, the actual Mona Lisa, but back before she'd had Arthur, which made it three decades ago, and it'd been hard enough even then to see anything of it because of the quite large mob of people standing in front of it taking its photo. It had also been remarkably small, the masterpiece, a lot smaller than she'd expected such a famous masterpiece to be. Maybe the crowd in front of it had made it seem smaller to the eye.

But the difference was that the people standing in front of it now were no longer even bothering to turn towards it. They mostly had their backs to it because they were taking pictures of themselves with it; these days that old painting was smiling in its superior way at people's backs, people with their phones held up above their heads in the air. The people looked like they were saluting. But saluting what?

The space in front of a painting where people stand and don't look at it?

Themselves?

The head on the table raised its eyebrows at her. As if it could read her mind, it gave her a little Mona Lisa smirk.

Very funny. Very smart.

National Gallery? Would it like the National Gallery? Tate Modern?

But all these places, if they were open at all today, would be closing at noon like most places and in any case the trains, Christmas Eve.

So. Not London.

What then? A walk on the clifftop?

But what if the head got blown out to sea?

Something hurt inside across her chest at the thought.

Whatever I do today you can come too, she said to the head. If you're good and quiet.

But I hardly need say that, she thought. I couldn't have a less obtrusive guest.

It's very nice, having you around the house, she said. You're very welcome.

Certainly the head looked happy with that.

Five days ago:

Sophia goes into the front room office, switches on her work computer, ignores the many emails with the red !s and goes straight to Google where she types in

blue green dot in eye

then, to be more precise,

blue green dot at side of vision getting bigger.

Do You Have a Spot on Your Iris? THIS is What it Means! -

Spots, Dots, and Floaters: Seeing What's Inside Your Eyes

When I close my eyes . . . I see colored dots : askscience

Blurred vision, Floating spots or strings in vision, Sensitive to light and

Seeing Colored Spots – Vision and Eye Disorders Forum – eHealthForum

5 Signs You have Retinal Migraine - Headache and Migraine News

Entoptic phenomenon – Wikipedia

She looks up a couple of the sites. Cataracts. Light filter problem. Vitreous detachment. Corneal abrasions. Macular degeneration. Floaters. Migraines. Possible retinal detachment. Seek prompt medical care if your spots or floaters are persistent or cause you concern.

Then she googles

seeing a little green-blue sphere off to the side of my vision.

Up comes The Art of Seeing: Third Eye Perception & The Mystical Gaze, a lot of stuff about psychics, and Why Seeing Lights is a Sign from Your Angels | Doreen Virtue - Official.

Oh for Christ sake.

She books an appointment in a couple of days' time at a chainstore optician in town.

The young blonde optician comes through from a back room and looks at the screen then looks at Sophia.

Hello Sophia, I'm Sandy, she says.

Hello Sandy. I'd prefer it if you'd call me Mrs Cleves, Sophia says.

Of course. Follow me please, S–, uh, the optician says.

The optician goes up a staircase at the back of the shop. Upstairs there's a room with a raised seat in it, much like at a dentist's, and various machines. The optician gestures to the seat to suggest to Sophia to sit in it. She stands at a desk making some notes. She asks when Soph– uh, Mrs Cleves – last visited an optician.

This is my first visit to an optician, Sophia says.

And you've come because you've been having a bit of trouble with your eyesight, the optician says.

That remains to be seen, Sophia says.

Ha ha! the young optician says as if Sophia is being witty, which she isn't.

The optician does distance reading tests and close-up reading tests, eye-blocking tests, tests where a puff of air hits the eyes, a test where she looks inside Sophia's eyes with a light that means Sophia is astonished (and unexpectedly moved) to be able to see a branchwork in her own blood vessels, and a test where you have to press a button to register when and if you see a dot as it moves round the screen.

Then she asks Sophia her birthdate again.

Gosh. I thought I might have written it down wrongly, the optician says. Because honestly your eyes are in such great shape. You don't even need reading glasses.

I see, Sophia says.

You do, the optician says, and really well for someone in your age demographic. You're really lucky.

Luck, is it? Sophia says.

Well, imagine it like this, the optician says. Imagine I'm a car mechanic and someone brings me in a car for a service, and it's a car from the 1940s, and I lift the lid and find the engine still nearly as clean as when it left the factory floor in (the optician checks her form) 1946, just amazing, a triumph.

You're saying I'm like an old Triumph, Sophia says.

Good as new, the optician (who clearly has no idea that a Triumph has ever been a car) says. Close as damnit to never been used. I don't know how you've done it.

You're inferring I've spent my life going around with my eyes shut, or been remiss in some way in fully using them? Sophia says.

Yes, ha, that's right, the optician says scanning the paperwork and stapling something to something. Criminal underuse of eyes, I'll have to report this to the eye authorities.

Then she sees Sophia's face.

Ah, she says. Uh.

Did you see anything at all in my eyes to concern you? Sophia says.

Is there something particularly concerning *you*, Mrs Cleves? the optician says. Something you're maybe not telling me or maybe worried about. Because underlying –

Sophia silences the girl with a dart of her (excellent) eyes.

What I need to know, and all I need to know, do I make myself clear, is, Sophia says. Did any of your machines indicate to you anything I should be worrying about as concerns my sight?

The optician opens her mouth. Then she shuts it. Then she opens it again.

No, the optician says.

Now, Sophia says. How much do I owe, and to whom do I pay it?

Nothing at all, the optician says. Because given that you're over sixty, there's no –

Oh, I see, Sophia says. That's why you re-checked my birthdate.

I'm sorry? the optician says.

You thought perhaps I was lying about my age. To get a free eye test out of your chainstore, Sophia says.

Um –, the young optician says.

She frowns. She looks down, looks suddenly lost and tragic among the chain's vulgar Christmas decorations. She doesn't say anything else. She puts the printouts and forms and the notes she's been making into a little folder which she hugs to her chest. She gestures to Sophia to proceed downstairs.

You first, please, Sandy, Sophia says.

The optician's blonde ponytail ups and downs as

she goes and when they reach the ground floor she disappears through the door she first came out of without a goodbye.

Similarly rudely, without looking up from the screen at the main desk, a girl behind the counter suggests to Sophia that she tweet, post on Facebook or leave a review on TripAdvisor about her experience at the optician's today as ratings really do make a difference.

Sophia opens the shop door for herself.

It's raining hard in the streets outside now and the optician's is the kind of place where they have golf umbrellas with the name of the chain on them, and there's an umbrella stand with some of these in it back by the desk. But the girl is looking at the screen and steadfastly not looking up at Sophia.

She gets to her car soaked through. She sits in it in the car park under the noise of rain on the roof, in the not unpleasant smell of wet coat and car seat. Drips run down her from her hair. It is liberating. She watches the rain change the windscreen to a moving blur. The streetlights come on and the blur fills with the misshapen shifting spots of many colours, like someone's thrown little paint-filled missiles at the windscreen; this is because of the municipal strings of coloured Christmas bulbs suspended round the edge of the car park.

The night is coming down.

But isn't it pretty? she says

and this is the first time she's spoken to it – the abrasion, degeneration, detachment, floater, which at this point is still fairly small, you can't yet make out it's a head, small as a fly floating about in front of her, a tiny sputnik, and when she speaks directly to it like that it's as if it's a ball hit by the steel lever at the side of a pinball machine and it ricochets from one side of the car to the other.

Its movement, at near four o clock in the winter dark on the shortest day of the year, is joyful.

In the dusk fade, before she turns the key to start the engine and drive home, Sophia watches it under the spill of colour on the glass, moving freely across the dashboard as if the dashboard's plastic is the surface of an ice rink, bouncing itself off the passenger headrest, tracing the curve of the steering wheel once, then again and again, like it's trying out its skill then showing off its skill.

Now she sat at the kitchen table. Now the whatever-it-was was the size of a real child's head, a smudged dusty child streaked with green, a child come home covered in grass-stains, a summer child in the winter light.

Would it stay child or become adult, the head? Would it grow up, so to speak, into the floating head of a fully grown human? Would it get even bigger than that? Size of a small bicycle wheel, the kind on folding bikes? Then the size of a full-size

bicycle wheel? of an old-fashioned beach ball? of
the inflatable globe of the world in the old film The
Great Dictator where Chaplin dresses as Hitler and
bats the world about in the air above him till it
bursts? Last night, as the head had amused itself
by bowling itself down the hall runner at the
cabinet to see how many of Godfrey's eighteenth
century English pottery figurines it could topple
each time by hitting itself off the legs of it, it
had looked for the first time like the rolling,
falling, cut-off, guillotined, beheaded, very real
head of a –

and this had been the point at which she'd
shut it out of the house, which wasn't hard,
because it was very trusting, the head. All she'd
needed to do was walk out into the garden in the
dark and it had followed her, she'd known it would,
bobbing like a helium balloon bought at a county
fair, and then, as it floated off ahead (a head) by
itself towards the leylandii as if it were actually
interested in shrubbery she'd ducked back into the
house and shut the door on it, she'd got herself
through the house as fast as she could and down
into the armchair in the front room, her head
down below the back of it so anyone (or thing)
looking in the window would think she wasn't
there.

Nothing, for half a minute, for a full minute.
Good.

But then at the window the gentlest tapping. Tap tap tap.

She'd stretched out low and got the remote off the side table, switched on the television and turned it up.

The news rolled round in its usual comforting hysteria.

But there underneath it again, tap tap tap.

So she'd gone through to the kitchen and put the radio on, someone on The Archers trying to find room in a fridge for a turkey, and behind the radio voices, on the sliding door out to the darkness of the garden, the tap tap tap.

Then at the little glass slot in the back door too, tap tap tappity.

So she'd gone upstairs in the dark, then upstairs again, then finally up the ladder through the hatch into the loft, across the loft room through the low door to the very back of the ensuite where she'd tucked herself under the handbasin.

Nothing.

The winter noise of wind in branches.

Then at the skylight a glow, like those nightlights for children afraid of the dark.

Tap tap tap.

It was there like a lit city clockface, winter moon on a Christmas card.

She came out from under the sink and opened the skylight and it came in.

First it floated level with her own head. Then it lowered itself to where the real head of a child would be and looked up at her with round hurt eyes. But immediately after this, as if it knew she'd despise it being pathetic or manipulative, it levitated level with her own head again.

It had a sprig of, was that holly in its mouth? It held it out to her like it was holding out a rose. She took the sprig. When she did, the head did a little air-shift and gave her a look.

What was it about that look that meant she carried the piece of holly down through all the floors of the old house, opened the front door and wove it through the doorknocker?

This year's Christmas wreath.

It is a Tuesday in the month of February in 1961, she is fourteen years old and when she comes down to breakfast Iris is up early – unbelievable, Iris out of bed on a day off – making toast for herself and being shouted at by their mother for getting ash in the butter, and then, like she just *fancies a walk* at eight fifteen in the morning Iris chums her to school and when they get to the gate just before she goes in, says, listen Philo, what time's your morning break? Ten past eleven, she says. Right, Iris says, tell some pal you're not feeling well, I mean choose a hypochondriac one and tell them you're feeling queasy today and I'll be waiting over there at

twenty past. She points across the road. See you!
and she flips her hand in a wave before Sophia can
ask anything, and two 4th year boys going past stop
and watch Iris walking away, one of them has his
mouth open, that really your sister, Cleves? the
other one says.

She bends over Barbara's desk at Maths.

You know, I feel quite sick today.

Oh dear, Barbara says and shifts well away
from her.

Iris, brilliant.

Iris, trouble. Sophia is not trouble, never trouble,
she is not a girl who ever does anything wrong, she
is pristine, correct, a girl clearly headed for head
girl (and head office, then head of her own business
ahead of the pack at a time when girls aren't meant
to be ahead or a head of anything, which will be the
first time in her life she finds herself quite so in the
wrong, and about which she'll inherit a fair level,
no, an unfair level, of guilt) and she's just
barefacedly lied, which has had the effect of
making her feel as queasy as she said she did, so it
was no lie after all then, and now she is about to do
something surely even more unallowed and wrong,
whatever it turns out to be, which makes her heart
beat so hard all through logarithms that she thinks
her whole self must be visibly beating, *please Sir,
Sophia Cleves seems to be throbbing*, but the break
bell goes and no one's said anything and she slips to

the girls' cloakroom and gets her coat off the hook, puts it on, does up the buttons as if she's going out into the cold though truly it's very warm today.

She stands near the Girls gate like she just happens to be standing there having a think about something, and she can see Iris over outside Melv's, the old tin Colman's Mustard sign up on the wall matching the yellow of Iris's coat as if Iris knew it would, wants it to.

Nobody is looking. Sophia crosses the road.

Outside the shop Iris stands guard between her and any passing housewifery who might report back to their mother, and she does as she's told, loosens her tie and rolls it into her pocket. Then Iris takes off her bright yellow coat and underneath it she's got on the butcher-boy leather jacket. She shoulders it off too and holds it out.

You can wear it till midnight tonight, Iris says, then you have to give it back or it turns to ashes and dust. Happy St Valentine's. Or call it an early Christmas present. Come on, try it on. Go on. There. God, Soph, you look a dream. Give's your coat.

Iris goes into Melv's with the school coat. She comes out without it. Melv says he'll keep it through the back for you till tomorrow, she says. But you'll have to get out of the house first thing without mother seeing you've no coat, so. Have an excuse ready.

What kind of excuse? she says. I can't lie to her like you can.

Me? a liar? Iris says. Tell her you left it at school. Too warm to wear it. Well! It's true.

It is true – it's meant to be winter still, February, but it's so warm, today it's shockingly warm, not just like in spring, more like summer. But she keeps the jacket on anyway all the way there, even on the Underground. Iris takes her to a coffee bar then to a place called Stock Pot for stew and potatoes, and then walks her round a corner and they're standing outside an Odeon. The poster outside is G.I. Blues. *Really?*

Iris laughs at the look on her face.

You're a picture, Soph.

Iris is a ban the bomb-er. No 'H' Bombs. No to Nuclear Suicide. From Fear To Sanity. Would You Drop an 'H' Bomb. Iris bought a duffel coat especially for the march, and the fight that started about the duffel coat became the biggest fight ever about anything, father furious with her, mother mortally embarrassed when she shocked the visitors at tea not just by holding forth, which in itself isn't on for girls to do, but by doing it about the poisonous dust in the air and in all the food now too then telling the people who came to the house from father's work about the *two hundred thousand people condemned to death in our name*, father hit her later when she shouted thou shalt not kill at him in the front room, and father never hits anyone. Iris has been saying for months that she'll never pay money to go to a film with Elvis playing a soldier in it. But she's even bought the good seats, balcony, as near the front as they can get.

In it Elvis is a soldier called Tulsa, an occupation GI out for the day with a dancer in Germany. The dancer is an actual German. If their father knew they were watching something in which Germans are seen as people he'd be as furious as when he stamped on the Springfields record and threw the pieces into the dustbin because of the where have all the flowers gone song in German on it. Elvis and the German dancer are on a ferryboat on the Rhine, a river which, she whispers to Iris, unusually happens to have its own private unit of measurement. (Iris sighs, rolls her eyes. Iris sighs too throughout Elvis singing to a baby in a basket a song about how the baby is already a little soldier, and Iris laughs out loud – the only person in the whole cinema who laughs – at the beginning of the film when Elvis, in a tank with a long protruding missile-firer, fires a missile that blows up a wooden shack, though Sophia can't see how or why this is funny, and at the end when they come out into the London streets Iris is shaking her head and laughing, a man like a melting candle, Iris says, melting candle of a man. How do you mean, Elvis is like a candle? she says. Iris laughs again and puts her arm round her. Come on, you. Coffee bar then home?)

There are so many songs in G.I. Blues that there is hardly a moment when Elvis is not singing something. But the best song happens when he and the German go to a park where there's a puppet theatre, like a Punch and Judy, in which a father puppet, a soldier puppet and a girl puppet are playing a scene to an audience of children. The girl puppet is in love with the soldier puppet and vice versa, but the father puppet says something like not a hope in German. So the soldier hits the father with a stick till the father's obliterated. The soldier puppet starts singing a German song to the girl puppet. But it goes wrong because the old man who runs the puppet theatre's record player starts playing the song wonky, too fast then too slow. So Elvis says *maybe I can get that thing going for him.*

Next thing that happens is, the whole cinema screen – and it's one of the widest she's ever seen, so much wider than the screens in town at home that it feels unfair – becomes nothing but the stage of the puppet theatre with Elvis in there visible from the chest up, a visiting giant from another world, next to him the puppet girl whole and tiny making him look like a kind of god. He starts to sing to the puppet and it becomes the most powerful, beautiful thing Sophia has ever seen; he is somehow even more beautiful and astounding than he was at the start of the film when he was in a shower with the other soldiers and soaping himself with no shirt on.

In particular there is a fraction of a second which later Sophia keeps trying to replay in her head but at the same time isn't completely sure she hasn't just imagined. But she can't have. Because it pierced her.

It comes when Elvis persuades the girl puppet, who is after all just a puppet but is somehow still also really funny and cheeky, to give in, lean herself back against his shoulder and chest for a moment. When she does this, he throws a look so small it's nearly not there to the girl he loves in the audience – and to the people watching the puppet show and also the people watching the film, which includes Sophia – the slightest gesture of his beautiful head as if to say, well, a great many things, among them: hey, look at this, look at me, look at her, who'd have thought? imagine that, see that?

Christmas Eve morning, 10am, and the disembodied head was dozing. Lacy green growth, leafy looking, a tangle of minuscule leaves and fronds, had thickened and crisped round its nostrils and upper lip like dried nasal mucus and the head was making the sounds of inhalation and exhalation in such a lifelike way that if anyone standing outside this room heard it he or she'd have been convinced that a real whole child, albeit one with a bad cold, was having a nap in here.

Would that stuff, Calpol, she could get some from the chemist's, maybe help?

But the same growth seemed to be coming out of its ears too.

How could it breathe anyway, the head, with no other breathing apparatus to speak of?

Where were its lungs?

Where was the rest of it?

Was there maybe someone else somewhere else with a small torso, a couple of arms, a leg, following him or her about? Was a small torso manoeuvring itself up and down the aisles of a supermarket? Or on a park bench, or on a chair by a radiator in someone's kitchen? Like the old song, Sophia sings it under her breath so as not to wake it, I'm nobody's child. I'm no body's child. Just like a flower. I'm growing wild.

What had happened to it?

Had what had happened to it hurt it very much?

It hurt her to think it. The hurt was surprising in itself. Sophia had been feeling nothing for some time now. Refugees in the sea. Children in ambulances. Blood-soaked men running to hospitals or away from burning hospitals carrying blood-covered children. Dust-covered dead people

by the sides of roads. Atrocities. People beaten up
and tortured in cells.

Nothing.

Also, just, you know, ordinary everyday
terribleness, ordinary people just walking around
on the streets of the country she'd grown up in, who
looked ruined, Dickensian, like poverty ghosts from
a hundred and fifty years ago.

Nothing.

But now she sat at her table on Christmas Eve
and felt pain play through her like a fine-tuned
many-stringed music and her the instrument.

Because how could losing so much of a self
not hurt?

What can I give it? Poor as I am?

Ah. That reminded her.

She checked the time on the cooker.

There'd be Christmas closing times at the
bank.

The bank.

Well. That did it

(money always does, always will)

and here instead's another version of what was
happening that morning, as if from a novel in which
Sophia is the kind of character she'd choose to be,
prefer to be, a character in a much more classic sort
of story, perfectly honed and comforting, about
how sombre yet bright the major-symphony of
winter is and how beautiful everything looks under

a high frost, how every grassblade is enhanced and silvered into individual beauty by it, how even the dull tarmac of the roads, the paving under our feet, shines when the weather's been cold enough and how something at the heart of us, at the heart of all our cold and frozen states, melts when we encounter a time of peace on earth, goodwill to all men; a story in which there's no room for severed heads; a work in which Sophia's perfectly honed minor-symphony modesty and narrative decorum complement the story she's in with the right kind of quiet wisdom-from-experience ageing-female status, making it a story that's thoughtful, dignified, conventional in structure thank God, the kind of quality literary fiction where the slow drift of snow across the landscape is merciful, has a perfect muffling decorum of its own, snow falling to whiten, soften, blur and prettify even further a landscape where there are *no* heads divided from bodies hanging around in the air or anywhere, either new ones, from new atrocities or murders or terrorisms, or old ones, left over from old historic atrocities and murders and terrorisms and bequeathed to the future as if in old French Revolution baskets, their wickerwork brown with the old dried blood, placed on the doorsteps of the neat and central-heating-interactive houses of now with notes tied to the handles saying *please look after this head thank you,*

well, no,
thank you,
thank you very much:

instead, it was Christmas Eve morning. It would be
a busy day. People were coming to stay for
Christmas, Arthur bringing his girlfriend/partner
with him. There was organizing to be done.

After breakfast Sophia drove to town, to the
bank, which stated on its website that it would be
open till noon.

She was still, regardless of the losses, what the
bank designated a Corinthian account holder,
which meant her bank cards had a graphic on them
of the top of a Corinthian pillar with its flourish of
stony leaves, unlike the more ordinary account
holder cards which had no graphic at all, and being
a Corinthian account holder meant she had the
right to personal treatment and attention at the
bank via an Individual Personal Adviser. For this
she paid more than £500 a year. For this, her
Individual Personal Adviser, should she ever have a
query or a need, was available to sit opposite her
and phone through to the bank's call centre for her
while she sat in the same room and waited. This
meant she didn't have to do this phoning herself,
though sometimes, all the same, the Individual
Personal Adviser simply wrote a number down on a
slip of bank paper and handed it to a client

suggesting it might be more comfortable for the client to do the phoning from home and this brush-off had also quite recently happened to Sophia, though she was, she believed, still well known, or at least, well, *known*, in the local bank as a once-stellar international businesswoman who'd come down here to retire.

Where were the bank managers of yesteryear? Their suits, their assurances, their knowing tips, their promises, their clever politesse, their expensive embossed personally signed Christmas cards? This morning the Individual Personal Adviser, a young man who looked to be about the age of a school-leaver and who, with Sophia sitting opposite him and the computer, was still on hold thirty five minutes later waiting for the bank's call centre to put him through to the right person without cutting him off, wasn't sure he'd be able to answer Mrs Cleves's queries before the bank closed at noon. It might maybe be better if Mrs Cleves made an appointment for after Christmas week.

The Individual Personal Adviser hung up the phone and booked Sophia a Personal Advice appointment slot on the computer for the first week of January. He explained to Sophia that the bank would send her an email confirming the appointment and then a text the day before as a reminder. Then – because the screen had clearly prompted him – he asked Mrs Cleves if she'd like to take out any insurance.

No, thank you, Sophia said.

Housing, buildings, car, possessions, health, travel, *any* kind of insurance? the Individual Personal Adviser said reading the screen.

But Sophia already had all the insurance she needed.

So the Individual Personal Adviser, still looking at the screen, told her some more facts about the competitive rates and the combination possibilities in the insurance range the bank could offer its premier customers. Then he checked through her Corinthian account details to tell her which of these insurances she already had, being a Corinthian card holder, and which of them her Corinthian account didn't cover.

Sophia reminded him that she'd like to take some cash out today before she left.

Then the Individual Personal Adviser began speaking about cash. Money, he said, was now being manufactured specifically for machines rather than for human hands. There would soon be a new ten pound note too, like the new five pound note, made of much the same stuff, materials which made it easier for machines to count notes, and a lot more difficult if you were a human being working in a bank to count them by hand. Soon, he said, there'd be almost no human beings left working in banks.

She saw a flush on the skin at his neck, up towards his ears. There was a flush on his cheekbones too. Probably the people working in this bank had started Christmas-party drinking early. He didn't look old enough to drink legally. He looked for a moment like he might actually start to cry. He was pathetic. His preoccupations were nothing to her; why should they be?

But Sophia, who knew from experience the uses of a good relationship with the people who work in banking, decided not to be impatient or unpleasantly sharp while the Individual Personal Adviser told her at a bit too much length about how he had found himself starting to choose the interactive checkout machine to avoid the now old-style real people who still ring purchases through at the supermarket checkouts.

At first he had been incensed, he said, when the supermarket where he buys his lunch took away some of the people working on checkout and replaced them with self-service checkout units. So he'd made a point of always choosing to pay a human being. But the queue for seeing a real person was always long because only one person was ever on those human tills now and the checkout machines were almost always free because there were more of them and therefore the queues for them moved so much faster and so he'd begun to go to the machines when he bought his lunch and now he always went straight to the machines and in a strange way it was a relief to because having a talk with someone, even the smallest, most casual of talks, was sometimes quite hard because you always felt they judged you or you always felt shy or that you were saying a stupid or wrong thing.

The pitfalls of human exchange, Sophia said.

The Individual Personal Adviser looked at her instead of his screen. She saw him see her.

She was some old woman he didn't know anything about or care about.

He glanced back at his screen. She knew he was looking at her account figures. Last year's figures weren't on there. They meant nothing. Nor the figures from the year before, or the one before that, and so on.

Where are the bank account figures of yesteryear?

It is a fact, Sophia said. The slightest human exchange is complex in the extreme. Now. If I may. I came in today specifically to withdraw a sum of cash.

Yes. My colleagues at the front desk will help you with today's cash withdrawal, Mrs Cleves, he said.

Then he looked at the screen and said, Oh no. No, I'm afraid they won't be able to.

Why? Sophia said.

I'm afraid we're now closed, he said.

36

Sophia looked at the clock on the wall behind him. Twenty three seconds past noon.

But you'll still be able to provide me with the amount I came in especially to take out today, Sophia said.

I'm afraid our safes lock automatically at close of day, the Individual Personal Adviser said.

I'd like you to check my client status, if you would, Sophia said.

We can check, he said, but it's unlikely we'll be able to do anything.

So what you're saying is, I can't withdraw the money I wish to withdraw out of my own account today, she said.

Of course you'll still be able to take out the amount you want up to your limit from the cash machine at the front of the bank, he said.

He stood up. He didn't do any status checking. He opened the door because their allotted time in this particular room and on this particular appointment was over.

Is there any chance I might discuss this with your branch manager? Sophia said.

I am the branch manager, Mrs Cleves, the Individual Personal Adviser said.

They wished each other a Merry Christmas. Sophia left the bank. She heard him lock the main doors behind her.

Outside the bank she went to the cash machine.

The machine had a message on its screen saying it was temporarily out of order.

Then Sophia got caught in the traffic jam congealing in all directions. She got caught next to the patch of grass in the centre of town, you could hardly call it a park, where that tree, all the years ago, used to have the white wooden bench round its trunk especially constructed to fit the girth of the tree but now had nothing. She thought momentarily about abandoning her car in the middle of the road and going to sit under the tree for a while, till the traffic cleared. She could just leave it in the middle of the road. The other people in cars could just drive round it. She could just sit on the turf.

She looked across at the great old tree.

She looked at the notice about the sale of the park and the plan for the *luxury flats office space prime retail space*. Luxury. Prime. In heaven the bells were ringing from a hardware, homeware and garden shop across the road from the green with a closing down sale banner across its windows. Gloh. Oh-oh-oh-oh-oh.

The thing about Christmas music that's particularly interesting, she thought to herself in a knowledgeable but not offputting Radio 4 voice as if on a programme about Christmas music, *is that it's thoroughly ineffectual, it just won't and doesn't work at any other time of the year. But now, at this bleakest midwinter time, it touches us deeply because it is insistent about both loneliness and communality*, she told the millions of listeners not listening. *It gives a voice to spirit at its biggest, and encourages spirit at its smallest, its most wizened, to soak itself in something richer. It intrinsically means a revisiting. It means the rhythm of the passing of time, yes, but also, and more so, the return of time in its endless and comforting cycle to this special point in the year when regardless of the dark and the cold we shore up and offer hospitality and goodwill and give them out, a bit of luxury in a world primed against them both.*

In the bleak silent night holy night above thy deep and dreamless sleep let nothing you dismay. She sighed, sat back into her seat. She knew them all – all the Christmas songs – didn't just know them, knew them word for word off by heart, plus descants. Perhaps *that* was what a Catholic indoctrination had been for, and the ancient old Welshman headmaster who took them for singing, remember him, the old head before the new younger head came, he was kindly, which made a change, and in between the singing he'd stop the class, arms out, hands open, like an old-time actor on a stage, and tell them stories instead of teaching anything. He was tweedy, bright-eyed, always had a certain scent all round him, medicinal, not unpleasant, and he was a man from a time so truly in the past to them that the whole class took him

and his stories as seriously as if they'd come direct
from God.

For instance he'd told them the one about the
famed artist who'd drawn nothing but a circle on a
piece of canvas with a piece of charcoal when the
emperor's messengers arrived, sent to him to
command him to paint for the emperor the world's
most perfect picture. *Give him this.*

What other stories had that old head told them?

This one.

*A man murdered another man in a stony field.
They'd had a disagreement about something and
one hit the other over the head with a big round
stone, a stone as big as a head. This killed the other
man. So the man who'd killed him scanned the
landscape all round them as far as he could
see to see if anyone might have seen it happen.
Nobody. He went home and got a shovel. He dug a
big hole in the field and rolled the dead man into it,
then he dropped the heavy stone over the side of a
bridge into the river. He went down to the side of
the river and washed himself and dusted down his
clothes.*

*But he couldn't get away from the thought of the
dead man's broken head. The thought of it
followed him wherever he went.*

*So he went to the church. Bless me Father, for I
have sinned. I fear God won't be able to forgive
what I've done.*

The priest, who was a young man too, reassured him that if he confessed and made a true good penance then of course he'd be forgiven.

I've killed a man. I've buried him in the cornfield, the man said. I hit him with a stone and he fell down dead. I dropped the stone I did it with into the river.

The priest nodded behind the darkened window, the little grille full of holes. He gave the man his penance and he said the words of Absolution. So the man went out and sat in the church and said the prayers and was forgiven.

Years passed, decades, and the whereabouts of the man who'd died ceased to concern or worry anyone. Everyone who cared had died and everyone else forgot him.

One day an old man met an old priest, by chance, on the way into town, and he recognized him and said, Father, shake me by the hand. I don't know if you remember me.

They travelled to town together and chatted about all sorts of things, family, life, the things that had changed, the things that had stayed the same.

Then, as they drew close to the town, the old man said, Father, I'd like to thank you for helping me all the years ago. I'd like to thank you for not telling anyone what I did.

What you did? the old priest said.

41

When I killed the man with the stone, the old man said, *and buried him in the cornfield.*

The old man took a flask out of his pocket and offered the old priest a drink. The priest drank a toast with the man. They nodded to each other and said goodbye when they arrived in the market square.

The old man went home. The old priest went to the police.

The police went to the cornfield and dug up some bones and they came for the old man.

The old man was tried, found guilty and hanged in the jail.

Riven with angels, the shops were shutting. The light of day was almost gone.

Sophia drove home. When she got home she unlocked the front door. She went through to the kitchen.

She sat down at the table.

She held her head in her hands.

On a late summer day in 1981 two young women are standing outside a typical ironmonger's on the high street of a southern English town. There is a sign above the door in the shape of a door key, on it the words KEYS CUT. There'll be a high smell of creosote, oil, paraffin, lawn treatment stuff. There'll be brushheads with handles, brushheads without handles, handles by themselves, for sale. What else? Rakes, spades, forks, a garden roller, a wall of stepladders, a tin bath full of bags of compost. Calor gas bottles, saucepans, frying pans, mopheads, charcoal, folding stools made of wood, a plastic bucket of plungers, stacked packs of sandpaper, sacks of sand in a wheelbarrow, metal doormats, axes, hammers, a camping stove or two, hessian carpet mats, stuff for curtains, stuff for curtain rails, stuff for screwing curtain rails to walls and pelmets, pliers, screwdrivers, bulbs, lamps, pails, pegs, laundry baskets. Saws, of all sizes. EVERYTHING FOR THE HOME.

But it's the flowers, *lobelia*, *alyssum*, and the racks of the bright coloured seed packets the women will remember most when they talk about it afterwards.

They say hello to the man behind the counter. They stand by the rolls of chains of different widths. They compare the price per yard. They calculate. One of them pulls a length of slim chain; it unrolls and clinks against itself, and the other stands in front of her pretending to look at something else while she passes the chain around her hips and measures it against herself.

They look at each other and shrug. They've no idea how long or short.

So they check how much money they've got. Under £10. They consider padlocks. They'll need to buy four. If they buy the smaller cheaper type of padlock it'll leave enough money for roughly three yards of it.

The ironmonger cuts the lengths for them. They pay him. The bell above the door will have clanged behind them. They'll have stepped back out into the town in its long English shadows, its summer languor.

Nobody looks at them. Nobody on the sleepy sunny street even gives them a second glance. They stand on the kerb. This town's high street seems unusually wide now. Was it this wide before they went into the shop, and they just didn't notice?

They don't dare to laugh till they're out of the town and back on the road walking the miles towards the others, and then they do. Then they laugh like anything.

Imagine them arm-in-arm in the warmth, one swinging the bag jangling the lengths of chain in it and singing to make the other laugh, jingle bells jingle bells jingle all the way, the other with the padlocks complete with their miniature keys in her pockets, and the grasses in the verges on both sides of the road they're on summer-yellow and shot through with the weeds, the wildflowers.

It is winter solstice. Art, in London, is on a worn-out communal pc in what was once the Reference bit of the library and now has a sign over its door saying Welcome To The Ideas Store. He is typing random words into Google to see if they come up automatically in frequent search as dead or not. Most of them do, and if they don't immediately come up as dead they pretty much always will if you type *[word]* plus *is* plus the letter *d*.

He has a little frisson of something – he isn't sure what, maybe masochism – when he types in *art* then *is* and up it comes, top answer on the top searches:

art is dead.

Then he tries the word masochism.

Masochism doesn't come up as dead.

Love, however, is definitely dead.

47

This place he's in is the opposite of dead. It is buzzing. It is full of people doing things. It was quite difficult to get a place on one of these old pcs and a lot of people are now standing waiting for one of the only five that are working. Some of the people in the queue have an urgent look like there are things they really have to do soon. One or two look frantic. They pace about behind the people in the pc cubicles. Art doesn't care. Today he doesn't care about anything. The famously gentle Art, the thoughtful generous lyrical sensitive Art, is giving way to no one else's needs and is staying in this makeshift fucking cubicle as long as he likes and as long as he chooses to.

(Out of *gentleness*, *thoughtfulness*, *generosity*, *lyricism* and *sensitivity*, only *lyricism* is *dead*.)

He has a lot of work to do.

He also has a blog piece to write about solstice and to upload before it isn't solstice any more.

He types in *blogs* and then *are*.

Up it comes. Dead.

He types in *nature is*.

It's one of the ones that need the extra *d*. When he adds it, up come these suggestions:

nature is dangerous

nature is dying

nature is divine

nature is dead

Nature writers, however, doesn't come up as

dead. When you type it in, a row of thumbnails comes up, little pictures of the healthy looking faces of all the greats, past and present. He looks at them, the little thoughtful faces, the world-understanders in their row of tiny online squares, and feels a terrible sadness at his core.

Can natures change?

Because his is feckless.

He is a selfish fraud.

Things never go so wrong, do they, in real nature writers' lives, that they can't solve it or salve it by writing about nature? And look at him.

Charlotte is right. He is not the real thing.

Charlotte.

His mother is expecting him and Charlotte in Cornwall in three days' time.

He takes his phone out of his pocket. He looks at its screen. Charlotte has started sending out fake tweets from @rtinnature. Yesterday, pretending to be him, she told his 3,451 followers that he'd seen the first brimstone of the new year cycle. *3 months early the first sieg hting of brimstone !* She is also making spelling mistakes on purpose to make him look stupid and slapdash and, considering that little *sieg*, maybe also trying to attract a few Nazis to the feed. She posted a picture she'll have downloaded off the net of a female brimstone on a leaf. Twitter went mad, mini twitterstorm, @rtinnature trended briefly because more than a thousand excited, angry and mildly abusive nature-loving people all took to castigating him at once for not knowing the difference between a new butterfly and a wakened hibernator.

Today's tweets, which began half an hour ago, also under his username, are telling everybody another blatant lie. Today Charlotte is tweeting pictures she's found somewhere of Euston Road in a snowstorm.

It isn't snowing. It's 11 degrees and sunny.

The replies are already foaming like badly poured lager. Fury and sarcasm and rancour and hatred and ridicule, and one tweet which said *if you were a woman I'd be sending you a death threat right about now*. Art is not sure whether this is a po-mo joke or not. Worse, a couple of media sources, an Australian one and an American one, have picked it up and run with it, with his twitter ID still on it. First Photos Central London Snowfall.

His phone in his hand lights up. *Dear Neph*.

It's Iris.

Yesterday Iris texted him to tell him the other meaning of brimstone. *Dear Neph, did u ever check out or cm across fire-and-forget function of so-calld Brimstone, I mean air-launched ground attack missile kind. Not very bttrfly eh! if *it* flaps wings then whole other bttrfly effect for sure x Ire*

Today she is unexpectedly comforting. *Dear Neph*, she says, *ur not soundng much like urself on twit :-$. So tell me now that u know persnlly : are we at mercy of tchnology or is tchnology at mercy of us? x Ire*

Well, that's brilliant. Because if even his aged old aunt who's into her what must be late seventies and in any case hardly knows him can tell he is being faked then he needn't worry, his true followers will definitely work it out.

Knee-deep snow in London tweeby mates!

He is not going to be drawn.

He is better than that.

He is not going to give her the pleasure of a stand-off.

He will not be brought so low.

He will allow her to reveal her own lowness by her actions.

(It is intriguing that Charlotte is so keen to keep in touch with him one way or another.)

He looks around him at all the people in the library. I mean, look. See that. Not one other person in this room knows or cares about the things that are happening online in his name and under his header photo. When you look at it like that it's pretty much like it isn't really happening.

Except it is.

So which is the real thing? Is this library *not* the world? Is *that* the world, the one on the screen, and this, this sitting here bodily with all these other people round him, *isn't*? He looks out the window beyond the boxy old pc screen. Traffic is passing, people passing in all directions, a girl is sitting reading something in a bus shelter opposite and she isn't in turmoil, is she?

No.

So he doesn't need to be.

But

tweeby mates

Charlotte is demeaning him and simultaneously making it look like he is demeaning his own followers. It is galling in so many ways. She knows it is. She is tweeting about snow specifically to be galling to him. She knows he has had everything planned, that he's been planning for quite some time for when it *does* properly snow, if it ever does again, for a piece about it for Art in Nature. He is – was – going to be riffing on the theme of footprints and alphabetical print. *Every written letter making its mark, digital or ink on paper, is a form of track, an animal spoor*, a line that's been in his notebook for well over a year and a half. She knows full well he's been waiting because of the warm winter last year. He has such good words now, great words to conjure with – trail, stamp, impress. He has also been collecting unusual words for snow conditions. Blenky. Sposh. Penitents. He is – was – going to get a bit political actually and talk about natural unity in seeming disunity, about how unity can be revealed against the odds by the random grace of snow's relationship with wind direction, the way that snow lands with an emphasis on one direction even though a tree's branches go in so many directions. (Charlotte thought this was a really lame idea and gave him a lecture about how he was missing the point, that all but the very best and most politically aware nature writers were habitually self-satisfied and self-blinding and comforting themselves about their own identities in troubling times, and that the word snowflake now had a whole new meaning and he should be writing about *that*.) He's been making notes on the give and take of water molecules, he was going to subhead it Generous Water. He's been noting why, on a cold day when there's very little breeze, something turning to ice will produce what looks like smoke, like a fire, and making notes about the combination of snow and ice called snice, with which buildings can be built because it's so strong, and about the feathery fernleaf shapes ice makes when it forms on some surfaces and doesn't on others, and on how it's actually *true* that no two snow crystals are ever alike, on the difference between flake and crystal and the communal nature of the snowflake – that's also quite a political thing to write about – as well as how flakes falling from the sky are their own natural alphabet, forming their own unique grammar every time.

Charlotte tore the pages out of the snow notebook and threw them out the window of the flat.

He'd looked out and seen what was left of them in the treetops and the bushes, on the windscreens and roofs of the cars parked beneath, blowing about on the pavement.

You, a nature writer, she said. Make me laugh. You can't just make up stuff about wandering around in a field or beside a canal and put it online and then call yourself a nature writer. In any case you're nothing but a grass. That's as close as you'll ever get to nature, grassing on people and taking a salary for it. Don't be thinking you can pass yourself off to people, or to yourself more like, as anything other than the scrappy patch of dishonourable grass you are.

They were having the fight because she'd caught him cleaning his fingernails out on the page edges of one of her books and had asked him not to, after which, because he was irked at being criticized, he'd started criticizing her endless moaning about the state of the world.

They made their choice, he said when she complained again about the people from the EU being made to wait to see if they can stay in the country or not, and people married to people from the EU, and people whose kids were born here who might not get to stay etc. They chose to come and live here. They ran that risk. It's not our responsibility.

Choice, she said.

Yes, he said.

Is this like when we were talking about the people who drowned trying to cross the sea running away from war, and you said we didn't need to feel responsible because it had been *their choice* to run away from their houses being burned down and bombed and then *their choice again* to get into a boat that capsized? she said.

This is the kind of thing she's been saying.

We're all right, he said. Stop worrying. We've enough money, we've both got good assured jobs. We're okay.

Your default to selfishness is not okay at all, she said.

Then she started shouting about the effect of forty years of political selfishness. As if you can talk about the effect of forty years of politics with any real knowledge when you yourself, if you're Charlotte, have only lived twenty nine. It is stultifying. No, what it is, really, is a form of self-hurt: witness the fact that Charlotte keeps talking about a recurring dream in which she is cutting herself open in a zigzag at the breastbone with a pair of chicken scissors, the bonecutting kind, then into four pieces like a chicken for soup.

In my dreams I'm a quartered kingdom, she has taken to saying whenever she wants attention. In my dreams I embody the terrible divisions in our country.

In her dreams is right.

The people in this country are in furious rages at each other after the last vote, she said, and the government we've got has done nothing to assuage it and instead is using people's rage for its own political expediency. Which is a grand old fascist trick if ever I saw one, and a very dangerous game to play. And what's happening in the United States is directly related, and probably financially related.

Art laughed out loud. Charlotte looked furious.

It's terrifying, she said.

No it isn't, he said.

You're fooling yourself, she said.

The world order was changing and what was truly new, here *and* there, Charlotte said, was that the people in power were self-servers who'd no idea about and felt no responsibility towards history.

That's not new either, he said.

They were like a new kind of being, she said – like beings who'd been birthed not by real historied time and people but by, by –

he watched her sitting on the edge of the bed with one hand on her collarbone and the other waving about in the air as she struggled for the right comparison –

By what? he said.

By plastic carrier bags, she said.

Eh? he said.

That unhistoried, she said. *That* inhuman. *That* brainless and unknowing about all the centuries of all the ways that people carried things before they were invented. *That* damaging to the environment for years and years after they've outgrown their use. Damage for generations.

It. Was. Ever, he said.

Then after a pause, he said, Thus.

How can you be so naive? she said.

After such an ultra-simplified anti-capitalist simile you're calling *me* naive? he said.

When pre-planned theatre is replacing politics, she said, and we're propelled into shock mode, trained to wait for whatever the next shock will be, served up shock on a 24 hour newsfeed like we're infants living from nipple to sleep to nipple to sleep –

A little nipple would be nice, now and again, he said.

(She ignored this.)

– from shock to shock and chaos to chaos like it's meant to be nourishment, she said. It's not nourishment. It's the opposite of nourishment. It's fake mothering. Fake fathering.

But why would they want to propel us from shock to shock? he said. What would be the point?

Distraction, she said.

From what? he said.

To make the stock markets volatile, she said. To make the currencies jumpy.

Conspiracy theory is so last year, he said. And the year before that. And the year before that. *Plus ça change.*

There's been *change* all right, she said (saying the word the French way like he had). Never mind literal climate change, there's been a whole seasonal shift. It's like walking in a blizzard all the time just trying to get to what's really happening beyond the noise and hype.

I'd love to chat all day about the seasons but I've work to do, he said.

He opened his laptop. He started looking up the sites where he might be able to buy up any remaining deodorant sticks of a certain make. The one he'd been using for years had been recently discontinued. She came across the room and hit the laptop screen with the back of her hand. She was jealous of his laptop.

I've the solstice blog to write, he said.

Solstice, she said. You said it. Darkest days ever. There's never been a time like this.

Yes there has, he said. The solstices are cyclic and they happen every year.

For some reason Charlotte really erupted at this. It is possible she's always hated his blog. In the fight, she called it his *irrelevant reactionary unpolitical* blog.

When have you ever even mentioned the world's threatened resources? she said. Water wars? The shelf the size of Wales that's about to break off the side of Antarctica?

The what? he said.

The plastic in the sea? she said. The plastic in the seabirds? The plastic in the innards of nearly every single fish or aquatic creature? Is there even such a thing left in the world as unruined water?

She had her arms up over her head, round her head as she said it.

Well, I'm just not a politico, he said. What I do is by its nature not political. Politics is transitory. What I do is the opposite of transitory. I watch the progress of the year in the fields, I look closely at the structures of hedgerows. Hedgerows are, well, they're hedgerows. They just aren't political.

She laughed in his face. She shouted about how very political hedgerows in fact were. Then furious rage came out of her, plus the word narcissist several times.

Art in Nature my arse, she said.

This was the point at which he'd left the room, then left the flat.

He'd stood out in the lobby for a bit.

She didn't come out to fetch him back in.

So he went downstairs to see what he could rescue of his snow notes.

When he came back up and into the flat he found

the hall cupboard door open, everything from its insides strewn across the floor and Charlotte choosing a drill-bit from the selection inside the flung-open drill-carrier. His laptop was flattened upside down suspended between two chairs. She held up the drill and pressed the trigger. It roared and whirred in the air.

Cue canned sitcom laughter.

What the fuck are you doing? he shouted over the whirr. You'll electrocute yourself.

She held up a large flat black thing.

Dead, she said. Like your political soul.

She tossed it at him spinningly like a Frisbee. Was that a laptop battery? Wow. How amazing the batteries in new laptops were, he thought as he ducked.

It clattered against the TV screen and he was lucky it missed him; such a thing looked like it could, at the right angle, decapitate.

(This was the moment he'd begun to suspect that Charlotte had maybe found the draft emails he'd been writing to Emily Bray about possibly meeting up on Wednesday evenings between four and six; he missed sex with Emily and had been drafting a letter to ask whether she missed sex with him too and whether some arrangement might be possible.

He'd never sent it.

He hadn't even been that sure he'd *ever* send it.

He'll write a new message to Emily. When he buys the new laptop.)

Political.

Soul.

He's already tried the word *politics*. It's dead.

Soul is d

Up comes the word dying.

Well, there's hope, then. Not dead yet.

Laptop is d

Up it comes, dead.

His laptop is definitely dead, its screen a mosaic of crazy paving, and Charlotte gone, her suitcases gone. Which is why he is here on a communal pc the keyboard of which makes the fingers on his hands feel as inept as some lovemaking sessions he'd rather not recall, and on which he can't find the key for the @.

He briefly considers contacting Emily Bray anyway to ask her if she'd like to come to his mother's with him for Christmas, because it will be feeble and embarrassing, since he has made such a fuss about bringing Charlotte, to turn up with nobody.

But he and Emily haven't spoken for nearly three years.

Since Charlotte.

He gets his phone out and looks through his contacts. No. Nope. No.

Then he laughs at himself for the outrageousness, the idiocy, of the idea.

He reads old Iris's text again.

Are we at the mercy.

No.

Come on.

He will survive this. Then – yes – he'll write about how he has survived it. He'll write a shining piece for Art in Nature about how to survive the fraudulent world, and not just how to survive it but how to get to the *truth* through it, through the pungent onion-layers of fraud (oh that's quite good, write it down Art), through even the lies told about you by your nearest and dearest and the lies you don't know you're telling yourself about yourself or others. He will cut through false narrative with razor edge writing. It'll be searing. It'll be honest. It'll be about what can't be taken from you. He will call it Truth Will Out. Or TWO.

The word TWO, though, makes him think of Charlotte again.

His heart sinks.

His phone in his hand starts to hum and buzz.

Maybe it's Charlotte!

No, it's a number he doesn't recognize.

He dismisses it.

Then another number he doesn't know is calling him. Then another.

He checks Twitter.

Sure enough, she's just posted a new tweet. The first thing he sees is a link. Above it:

Just lettin you all know I charge £10 a snow-job
or £5 mates rates for followers

He clicks on the link. It takes him to a page with a picture of him on it raising a glass of wine on their holiday to Thailand last year. There's a number underneath.

It's his phone number.

Oh God.

He switches his phone off.

He looks all round him to see if anyone's looking at him. Some people in the queue for using the pcs *are* looking at him but only because he's turned away from the screen and they're hoping he'll be leaving.

But his world is in meltdown!

He puts his hand to the nape of his neck. He is sweating.

Is a snow-job a sex thing?

What do people do to each other when they do a snow-job?

He looks it up online. Definitions come up straight away on this public screen so it can't be anything too obscene.

It seems to be something to do with G.I. Joe.

Okay.

He puts his off phone in his pocket, pushes the chair back and goes to the Gents.

In the Gents, behind the only lockable working door, he sits and stares at the floor. But it is horrible in here, smells foul and there's nothing to see. If this is privacy it effects nothing.

He gets up and unlocks the door.

When he comes out there's a woman in the Gents. She is quite young, twenties, South American maybe, dark hair, maybe Spanish or Italian. She is warming her chest, the bare tops of her breasts, in the air from the hand-dryer nozzle; she has turned the nozzle sideways towards her. She is wearing quite a low top for December. She gestures to it and to the dryer.

Cold. Warm. Forgive me, she says over the noise. The one in the Ladies is kaput.

I forgive you, he says.

She smiles and curves back towards the airflow and as he leaves the Gents he feels a bit better for just seeing another person, just having a passing exchange with another person, seeing someone doing such a lovely natural warm and warming thing.

Just saying out loud the word forgive. He hadn't known it was such a powerful word. He is smiling. People who walk past him on the stairs look at him like he's weird because he's smiling. None of them smiles back. He doesn't care. As he crosses the landing towards the Ideas Store he wishes he'd thought to ask *her*, that warm-breasted smiling girl, if she'd like to come with him to his mother's for Christmas.

Ha ha. Imagine.

But a man with a face that's all furrows is sitting

in the seat Art was formerly in and working at the keyboard, and a woman with three very young children hanging off her arm and legs is folding Art's coat neatly on top of his notebook and briefcase on the floor beyond the cubicle.

Fair enough. Art nods to the woman, who looks tireder, he thinks, in this blatant revealing Ideas Store striplight, than anyone he's ever seen.

Thank you, he says.

He means for folding the coat. But she looks right through him, maybe in case he's being sarky because the man she's with has taken his seat, in fact she looks like she's going to swear at him or give him hassle, so he picks up his stuff, goes towards the doors, stops at the main desk where he borrows a biro on a string from the woman there and writes the words *blatant* and *revealing* with it on the back of his hand.

Nothing is lost. Nothing is wasted. See, Art? Always half full.

Half fool. (Charlotte, in his ear.)

He leaves the building through the side door; the old front entrance of the library building is reserved for the people who live in the luxury flats in the rest of the building now. But he can't get angry about that, it is a waste of valuable energy to get angry about the kind of thing you can't do anything about, the kind of thing Charlotte goes on and on about. Thinking about Charlotte is also a waste of valuable energy and to free himself from it and from her he is now going to go out into the streets of this city and find, wherever he can, a handful of earth

(is dying
is divided into twenty four
is doomed
is destroyed
is dead)

so as ceremonially to hold in his hand nothing but soil, a handful of it breathing at its own rate, slow and meditative and completely itself through all the anger and the rot, earth itself, to remind him of it stilling to hard and frozen when the temperatures fall and thawing back to pliant again when they rise. That's what winter is: an exercise in remembering how to still yourself then how to come pliantly back to life again. An exercise in adapting yourself to whatever frozen or molten state it brings you. So gentle Art will look for literal earth. City earth. He'll look in the places where the city trees meet the pavement; sometimes there are patches of earth round them if they haven't been rubbered-in under that bouncy plastic stuff. Nature is adaptable. Nature changes all the time.

When he comes out on to the high street he sees a girl. It is the same girl he saw from the window nearly three hours ago. She is still at the bus stop. She's sitting in exactly the same place still reading something. She is reading whatever it is very assiduously.

He watches a bus pull up and stop, pick some people up, then indicate out and continue.

He watches another bus indicate, stop, then pull away again. As it does, there she is, still sitting, still reading.

She looks like she's about nineteen. She is quite pretty. She looks pale. She looks a bit rough. But the thing she most looks is concentrated.

Nobody has focus like that when they're just sitting at a bus stop.

He forgets about the earth.

He crosses the road and stands along from the bus shelter. He can see from here what it is she's reading. It's a take-away menu, a junk mail leaflet for a fast food place. He comes closer until he can make out the words FREE, DELIVERY, VARIETY and BUCKET.

She is reading a Chicken Cottage menu.

She reads the front of the leaflet. She opens the leaflet out. She reads it from one side to the other. She folds it closed and reads the back with the attention you'd give a good book.

When she finishes the back she turns it over to read the front again.

It is Christmas Eve morning three days later.

It is twenty minutes later than their agreed meeting time.

The girl isn't here.

67

There's no girl or young woman anything like her waiting anywhere near the place he suggested by the rows of seats in front of the information boards.

So she hasn't turned up.

So she's not coming, then.

Good. It is a relief.

It was a really really stupid idea and he has been regretting it.

Plus, he'll save the £1,000, money he'd prefer not to waste on an experiment really.

He will brave it out with his mother when he gets there. Or make something up: *poor Charlotte, she was really ill. I've never seen her so ill.* [Then why did you, how could you, leave her?] *Oh no, she's at her mother's, gone to her mother's for Christmas.* Or better: *her mother's come down to London especially to look after her so I could still spend this Christmas with you.*

He gets himself a coffee then scans the people waiting on and around the seats. He walks round a couple of times, checks again just in case.

Not that he can really remember what she looks like; it's not as if they've known each other for longer than a sandwich.

He can't phone her because she told him she doesn't have a phone.

Probably a bad idea anyway to think to hook up in any way with the kind of person who hasn't got a phone.

He settles into himself.

He stops feeling that way you do when you're acting differently because you know you're being seen from the outside.

But then he sees, way off in the distance, someone so unmistakeably the girl that he is almost shocked at how it couldn't be anybody other than her.

She appears and disappears, a still point in the churning crowd on the Heathrow Express ramp with their luggage and their tubes of wrapping paper, their plastic bags; she is standing looking up at the station roof as the people go up and down the ramp all round her.

Art hurries to the machine queue to buy her her ticket, so as not to seem rude and do it in her presence. When he's bought it there's not much time left. He goes to the designated meeting place, the rows of chairs. But there's no sign of her.

He looks across the concourse again. There she is, still standing on the ramp.

What she seems to be looking at so keenly, he finds when he goes to fetch her (because the train leaves in under fifteen minutes), is some old metal curlicues in the design of the station windows.

He stands at the bottom of the ramp. He jiggles his coffee cup from hand to hand. She still doesn't see him.

He pushes up the ramp through the people coming down.

Oh, hi, she says.

Is this, like, Travel Light Day? he says. Because if it is, I don't think anyone else in this station got the notification. Where's your luggage?

I uh didn't know whether to get you a coffee, he says. I didn't know how you'd take it.

You have the seat, he says on the train. I like standing. I can sit on the floor, no worries. I'll sit on the floor.

Oh, I work for SA4A Ents, he says. It's the entertainment division of SA4A. SA4A. You know, SA4A. I can't believe you haven't heard of them. They're huge, they're everywhere. I'm a copyright consolidator. It means I check through all forms of media, online and offline, films, visuals, things in print, soundtrack, everything really, for copyright infringement, any unlawful or uncredited quotation or usage, and report back to SA4A Ents when I find anything out of place or not credited so they can chase up rightful payment or issue the lawsuits. And if they've actually credited SA4A I check it's all shipshape. What? No, I work from home. Oh. Ha ha. No, shipshape means, like, properly ratified, legally done. It's never boring plus I'm my own boss. My own hours, middle of the night if I want, it's all on my own terms, which is basically why I do

70

it. Also, it does mean I get to watch loads of things. I see all sorts of things I'd otherwise never in a million years.

Peanuts? he says. So does that mean you have to wear like special hygienic clothes, or if you go on a train you have to announce yourself so people with nut allergies will know not to travel anywhere with you near them? Oh. Those. Those things're really bad for the planet. I really dislike them. On principle. I mean, being someone who really cares about the planet. Well. Well, if you say so.

If you don't mind me asking, he says. How old are you?

Again, don't mind me, he says, old-fashioned guilty as charged, but all the, the piercings? I mean, I get it, yeah, but so many?

Actually I should explain that my mother's a bit of a character, he says. She's hugely – you could say anally – tidy, into tidiness. She's a bit older than you might expect, she had me quite late, she's a shoes off at the front door kind of person. Things clean and neat, people clean and neat, well I mean I like clean and neat too, but she's what you'd call full-on.

Do I need luggage? she says.

I wouldn't have minded at all, she says. Why would I take you buying me a coffee the wrong way? Oh, I get it! ha ha! I like it naked. You just blushed, did you know? Okay, for future ref, I like it with nothing in it. Anyway I don't need one right now but thanks.

But you're paying, she says. No, I'm the employee, *I'll* sit on the floor. No, I don't mind. I don't mind! I really don't. Look, we both can, what about we both do? Space by those bags in the corridor. Come on. Yeah?

Who're they? she says. A what? You work on a ship? Oh. Shipshape. Ha ha!

I work at DTY, she says. Half the day I pad deliveries out with peanuts, the other half I pick up the peanuts that've fallen on to the floor and put them back in the basins. It beats standing at a stall selling no soap to anybody in a shopping centre twelve hours a day. No, no, not, like, real nuts – packing filler, it's what packing filler gets called, peanuts, we call them it anyway. Those green things, white things, polystyrene. You're wrong, they're recyclable. They're free of whatever it is that's bad for it. It's not as bad as you'd think. I quite like them. I do! No, it's interesting, because, because they're so amazingly light, so that when you pick them up it's surprising every time. You always expect them to be heavier. Even if you tell yourself, even though you know they're light, you think you already know, you pick one up and it's like, wow that's so light, it's like holding actual lightness. It's, like, the weight of your own hand just somehow got lighter. Like a bird's bones kind of light. If you pick up several, hold several so your hand's full of them, you look at your hand loaded with things and your eye can't understand it because although you can see that your hand's full of something it feels like almost nothing's in your hand.

Wow, you really *are* old-fashioned, she says. I'm twenty one. Special occasion so I've got them all in. Don't you have any other friends with piercings? Okay, no worries. I'll take them all out when we get there.

So anyway, she says, you better maybe tell me some things about who it is I'm meant to be being again. What's her name?

For a whole hour and a half, Art realizes, he hasn't thought once about her.

Charlotte.

Her name's Charlotte, he says.

He laughs to himself.

What's funny? the girl says.

Funny to be doing this, he says, and not yet know *your* name. And you don't know mine either.

Maybe we don't need names, she says. Anyway, I'm Charlotte now.

Okay, he says. But truthfully. I'm Art.

What, really? she says. Art?

Well, short for Arthur, he says. After the, you know, king.

Which king's that again? she says.

You don't really mean that, he says.

Don't I? she says.

You know who King Arthur is, he says.

Do I? she says. Anyway. Truthfully, I'm Lux.

You're what? he says.

As in el then you then ex, she says.

Lux, he says. Really?

Short for Velux, she says. After, the, you know. Window.

You're making that up, he says.

Am I? she says. Anyway. Help me make up Charlotte. I need a lesson in Charlotte.

He tells her his mother's never met Charlotte. So basically, Charlotte can be anyone.

She can even be me, she says.

That's not what I meant, he says.

He blushes and she sees.

Touchy, is she, your Charlotte? she says. Bit sensitive?

The bane of my life, he says.

Then why would you want to take her home in the first place? she says. Why wouldn't you just tell your family the truth, that she's the pain of your life –

Bane, he says.

– and that you don't want to bring her so you just decided not to? she says.

If you don't want this employment, uh, Lux, he says (with that pause at using her name because he is asking himself inside his head whether it's her real name or whether she's just made up a name off the top of her head). I mean, I won't mind at all if you've changed your mind. There's a station stop in about quarter of an hour and I'll gladly cover your return fare to London. If there's something about the arrangement that doesn't suit you.

She looks momentarily panicked.

No no, she says. We agreed. Three full days, £1,000. Which, by the way, works out as – I worked it out – just under £14 an hour, and if you decided on the Tuesday after we're done to pay me just an extra £8, just £8 more on the 27th, I mean if you pay me £1,008 in the end, that'd make it a round £14 per hour. Which is a lot neater than the amount per hour otherwise.

He says nothing.

Not that I'm not completely fine with your original offer of the thousand, she says.

I feel a bit bad, he says. I'm stopping you having, I'm taking you away from, your own family Christmas.

She laughs like she thinks what he's said is really funny.

My family are out of the country, she says. Don't feel bad. Think of it like, like I'm, I don't know, working in the hotel trade. Which means I'll have this fantastic Christmas after Christmas, and when your Christmas is finished and gone I'll be still having mine, and I'll be doing it with the salary you pay me for working over Christmas.

The money thing feels weird, he says.

She smiles charmingly.

Deal, she says. Fair and square. Helps me, helps you. And if your mother's never met your Charlotte, then it's easy. I mean, I might like a few pointers. Like, is your Charlotte clever or stupid? Is she kind or not? Does she like animals? That kind of thing.

Your Charlotte.

Charlotte, clever.

Charlotte, stupid.

Charlotte, kind.

He looks at the girl next to him, a stranger saying Charlotte's name.

Charlotte, beautiful. More beautiful than anyone. More full of feeling and understanding than anyone he's ever. Charlotte's back, Charlotte on the bed with her beautiful bare back, the line of her spine turned towards him. Charlotte, stunning. Other words for Charlotte? Musical. Thoughtful. Always catching him out with her sidelong consciousness, her way of listening to the sides of what you say and responding to what you didn't know you were saying, or to what you were trying but failing to say. Her complete lack of self-knowledge. Her laughably sincere university dissertation about the lyrics of Gilbert O'Sullivan: *Ooh Wakka Doo Wakka Day:*

76

language, semiotics and presence in 1970s mainstream entertainment. Her handwriting. Her perfume. Her detritus of necklaces and bangles. Her bulge of a make-up bag in the bedside cabinet, the smell of her make-up. Her passionateness, her passion for all sorts of things. Her taking the world so personally. Her endless hurt and fury at the world's sadnesses, like they're personal, personally meant, personal affronts. Her endless feeling. Her endless feeling for everything. Her endless feeling for everything except him. Charlotte, tiresome. Charlotte, maddening. Charlotte doing that maddening thing, always stopping to speak to just any cat she's seen in the street, in any street, here, there, in Greece on holiday, anywhere she sees a fucking cat getting down on her haunches and stretching her hand out like Art's not there, like the cat won't want to speak to him anyway even if he is, like the whole world has shifted to just her and some cat she doesn't even know like she's the only person in the whole world with any animal magnetism.

Charlotte, taking the special screwdriver he needed with her when she left, on purpose, so he couldn't put his laptop back together to find out whether anything on it could be rescued without going out and buying another of those screwdrivers.

He leans back against whoever's rucksack is behind him.

How to describe Charlotte, he says.

But he doesn't have to describe her after all because the girl, the woman, Lux, has fallen asleep with her head on her arms on somebody's suitcase.

He is moved by the trust. It takes trust to fall asleep with someone you don't know.

Then he is moved by his own being moved.

Narcissist. She's asleep because she's so not interested in you. (Charlotte, in his ear.)

He wonders if he'll end up sleeping with her narciss—

she is thin and wiry. Her body looks younger than she says she is. Her head looks bigger than it should. Her wrists have the thinness of the child she isn't far from having just been, her ankles above her boots are bare and their thinness is moving, in an upsetting way. Her face, glinting metal, toughened, suggests she's a lot older. Her clothes are clean but worn. Her hair is clean but dull. Now that she's asleep she looks exhausted. She looks like she hasn't had enough to eat for too long. She looks like sleep's punched her in the gut and dropped her into this train carriage corridor from a great height.

He'd asked her why she was sitting out in the cold and not in the warm library across the road. She told him she'd had a difference of opinion with the woman behind the Ideas Store desk. What about? he said. That's between me and her, she said. He'd offered, at the bus shelter, to buy her something off the Chicken Cottage menu. And spoil my perfect imaginings with the reality? she said.

He wonders if he looks nice in this turtleneck.

He'd check what he looks like on his phone, if it didn't involve putting his phone on.

Narcissist.

He shakes his head. He has no idea what he's doing. A girl like a broken bird.

St Erth! she'll say in a couple of hours as they draw into the station and she sees the signs. They've spelled it wrong! she'll say.

And: when do we get to see the wall?

Which wall? he'll say.

Of corn, she'll say.

And: it looks like old postcards here, she'll say as the train pulls out along the coast. Like cards from the past with the faded colours. Is that a castle? Is this place real? Did you grow up round here? No, he'll say, I grew up in London, but my mother bought her house here a couple of years ago, I haven't even seen it yet, but my mother's sister used to live down here I think and maybe she sent me books or something when I was a kid because I know there's a lot of lore, stories about the landscape being made of sleeping giants and such like, and I know it's a place whose own language is ancient and apparently won't ever die out, always resists, comes back even when it seems to be fading, won't ever be killed off by anything. You know, specific local language. Idiolect.

What did you just call me? the girl will say.

Then she'll raise an eyebrow at him because she's caught him out underestimating her, a laugh will come out of his mouth and as they draw into the station Art will catch himself laughing at his own preconceptions.

The bus service, it says on the noticeboard, has been permanently discontinued.

It takes an hour and a half to get a taxi. Then, because of Christmas traffic, it takes another hour and a half for the taxi they eventually get to drop them off at the gate in the dark.

In it, on the way, the girl removes her ear bars, her nose and lip rings, the studs, the little chain connecting her nostril and her lip.

CHEI BRES, it says on the sign at the gate.

What does it mean? the girl says.

No idea, Art says.

A house called No Idea, the girl says.

The walk from the gate to the house is unexpectedly far and the path is muddy after the storm. He puts his phone on to light the way. It buzzes with Twitter alerts as soon as he puts it on. Oh God. So much for low reception. He worries about what the alerts might be alerting him to, then deflects that worry by worrying about his boots and about remembering to stress to the girl to take her own boots off when they get to the front door of the house, which is clearly just over there, lit-up behind the hedges.

But then they round the corner and see that the light isn't house light, it's car light, and they find a car strewn in the middle of the road with its driver's door hanging open outside an outbuilding whose doors are also wide open.

Is this it? the girl says.

Uh, Art says.

He feels about on the inside wall of the building. When the fluorescent tubes blink on he sees that the place, which is huge, goes back much further than just a garage and is full of boxed-up stuff.

Stock storage, he says. My mother's chain of shops.

What kind of shops? the girl says.

She's pointing at the old lifesize foyer cardboard cut-out of Godfrey over against a wall standing with one hand on a hip and the other in a flourish at what's written above his head in the rainbow arch: *Godfrey Gable says: Oh! Don't Be Like That!*

Ah. Art says. That's my father.

The girl obviously doesn't recognize Godfrey. Well, she wouldn't. She's way too young to. If Godfrey hadn't been his father, he probably wouldn't recognize him either.

(Charlotte hadn't just known who Godfrey was, she even had a vinyl copy of one of the radio recordings, though no turntable to listen to it on, when he'd first met her. She'd known more about Godfrey, when Art met her, than Art himself did.)

Wild, the girl says.

Long story, Art says. Daddy I hardly knew him.

You say such weird things, the girl says.

I only met him twice, Art says. He's dead now.

That does the job, stops her in her tracks saying the word weird at him; she looks at him with the right kind of sad face instead.

He switches the light off in the barn, sits in the driver's seat in the car and finds the headlight switch. Off. Everything goes dark.

This building, *and* all this land, and you're telling me there's also a house as well? the girl is saying.

They follow the path to get to the house. It looms out of the darkness at them in darkness itself. Its front door is wide open and the inside door beyond it too.

Take your shoes off, he says.

While he's pulling his own boots off the porch lights up, then the hall lights up. He walks over the unopened Christmas cards in his socks. The girl is going ahead of him finding the light switches; a living room off the hall lights up. The level of heat in here is high. A lounge lights up. It's very hot in there.

He opens a door and finds a small room with a toilet and washbasin. He washes his hands.

He crosses the hall past the cabinet full of the

priceless ceramics. Godfrey's. They're skewy, some are broken, most are lying on their sides or on top of and under each other like a meteor has hit their world.

He comes into a huge kitchen. The girl is here, already sitting opposite his mother at the table. There's an Aga giving off immense heat. The radiator he touches on his way in is so hot the touch is close to a burn. But his mother is wearing a buttoned-up coat, a scarf, sheepskin gloves and a fur hat of a thickness that makes her head look animal.

She is staring ahead under the fur as if there's nobody here but her.

Is this your mother? the girl says.

Art nods.

He looks around for a boiler or a thermostat. He can't find either. He opens the fridge. There is almost nothing in it. There's a jar of mustard half empty, a single egg, an unopened packet of salad the insides of which are brown sludge. He looks inside a large cupboard. It has a couple of coffee packets. A tub of organic bouillon. An unopened packet of walnuts.

He comes back to the table. Two apples and a lemon in a bowl. He sits down.

Is this not normal, then? the girl says.

Art shakes his head.

The girl bites a fingernail.

Are you planning going out somewhere cold? she says to his mother.

His mother makes a noise, impatient and sarky and dismissive all in one grunt.

I'll call a doctor, Art says.

His mother raises a warning glove.

You will call a doctor, Arthur, she says, over my dead body.

The girl gets up. She lifts the hat off his mother's head. She puts it on the table.

You're far too hot, she says to his mother.

She loosens the scarf and takes it off and folds it, puts it in front of his mother on the table next to the hat. She bends round and undoes the buttons of the coat and shakes it open at his mother's shoulders. But she won't be able to get the coat off his mother without removing the gloves and his mother now has her massive sheepskin hands firm-clasped.

Would you like to take off your gloves as well? she says.

No, thank you, his mother says. But thank you very much.

Take them off, Sophia, Art says. This is my partner. Charlotte.

It's nice to meet you, the girl says.

I'm very, very cold, is all his mother says.

She shrugs her shoulders inside the coat so the coat closes over at her neck again.

Okay, the girl says, well. If you're cold.

She opens cupboards till she finds a glass, which she fills with water from the tap.

I wonder if you're aware, if you know, his mother says taking the glass of water in her sheepskin paw, that your face is full of little holes.

I do know, the girl says.

I also wonder if you know how unwelcome you are here, his mother says. I'm unusually busy this Christmas and won't have time for entertaining guests.

No, I didn't know that till now, the girl says, but now I do.

In fact, it's so hectic this year you may have to sleep in the barn rather than the house, she says.

Anywhere will do, the girl says.

No it won't, Art says. She can't. Sophia. We can't. Sleep in a barn.

His mother ignores him.

My son has, in passing, told me about your virtuoso status on the violin, she says.

Ah, the girl says.

So given that you're here you may as well entertain me at some point, his mother says. I'm very fond of the arts. I don't know if he's told you that.

Oh, I'd be far too shy to play anything for you, the girl says.

Self-deprecation is almost always distasteful, his mother says.

No, I can honestly say I'm honestly going to be nowhere near as good at playing a violin as you imagine, the girl says.

Well, there's nothing else I need to know about you right now, his mother says.

Thanks, the girl says.

You're welcome, his mother says.

No I'm not, the girl says.

Ha! his mother says.

His mother actually almost smiles.

But then she closes her face again, sits there staring at whatever nothing she's staring at in her outdoor clothes and the girl steps back, polite, and goes and stands in the hall. She beckons to Art from the door but his insides have become a kind of frozen. All he can do is stand in the wings of whatever the drama is. His head is empty, like everything has drained out of it, as in the old song about the hole in the bucket, dear Liza, which is all that's inside him right now, an ole. *Well mend it, dear Henry.* How can you mend an ole with a straw? He has never understood that song. Unless the ole is very very small. Right now the ole in im is too big for that, and this song playing through him in its comedy regional voice has turned him into a bit-actor on the stage of his mother's life. Again.

He looks at the long-dead flowers in the vase on the table. Perhaps that's where the smell in here is coming from. They make him even more furious with his mother, who tonight is outdoing any previous performance of herself. She is surpassing herself.

He looks at the strange girl in his mother's house. He has been an idiot to bring anyone, an idiot to come, himself, at all.

Not an idiot. An idiolect. That's what he is, a language no one else alive in the world speaks. He is the last living speaker of himself. He's been too blithe, he'd forgotten for a whole train journey, for almost a whole day, that he himself is dead as a disappeared grammar, a graveyard scatter of phonemes and morphemes.

He makes a supreme effort. He walks across the room to the girl at the door. The girl takes him by the arm.

Is there someone you can call? the girl says.

She is saying this quietly so his mother won't hear. She is being kind. Her kindness makes him flinch nearly as much as his mother's coldness.

I'll call that taxi back, he says. I'll call another taxi. It can take us to, to, I don't know. There are hotels in the town, I can call a hotel. I can try and call us a taxi to get us back to London, but I, I think, given it's Christmas Eve, and how late now, we might have to wait till –

Don't be a silly wanker, the girl says.

I'm not a –, he says but the girl puts her hand up, she isn't listening.

The sister, she says.

What? he says.

You said there's a sister. Does she live near here?

He moves the girl slightly further out into the hall with his big blunt hands.

We have to call the sister, the girl says.

I can't, he says.

Why not? the girl says.

They don't speak, he says. They haven't spoken to each other for nearly three decades.

The girl nods.

Phone her, she says.

January:

it is a reasonably balmy Monday, 9 degrees, in late winter a couple of days after five million people, mostly women, take part in marches all across the world to protest against misogyny in power.

A man barks at a woman.

I mean barks like a dog. *Woof woof.*

This happens in the House of Commons.

The woman is speaking. She is asking a question. The man barks at her in the middle of her asking it.

More fully: an opposition Member of Parliament is asking a Foreign Secretary a question in the House of Commons.

She is questioning a British Prime Minister's show of friendly demeanour and repeated proclamation of *special relationship* with an

American President, who also has a habit of likening women to dogs, and who has announced, on a day marked in calendars as Holocaust Memorial Day, that he intends to prohibit entry into the United States of America to large swathes of people based on their faith and ethnicity.

While the Member of Parliament is speaking, on the one hand bringing up the impact of this planned ruling on the refugee crisis and on people in forced exile from the war in Syria, and on the other asking a serious question about what leadership itself might mean both here and in the United States, a governing senior Member of Parliament barks at her like a dog.

Woof woof.

Some trivia: the House of Commons is one of the two Houses of Parliament in the United Kingdom, the UK's twin bodies of legislative supremacy.

The female MP is a law graduate and also happens to have been a bit of a TV star in Pakistan, having spent years before her time in the House of Commons acting in a popular drama series shown there.

The male MP is a former stockbroker and a grandson of Winston Churchill.

Afterwards, when the female MP complains, the male MP apologizes. He suggests it was lighthearted banter.

The female MP accepts his apology.

Both are gracious about it.

It's winter, still. There's no snow. There's been almost none all winter. It'll be one of the warmest winters on record, again.

Still, it's colder in some places than others.

This morning there was frost on the ridges of the turned earth across the fields, frost the sun had melted on one side only.

Art in nature.

2

Now it's the dark of early Christmas morning, the time before dawn, and this is the best time in the world for an old song about a lost child travelling in the snow.

(But who was the child in the song? Where was the child going? Why was the child out in the snow at all? Was the child really cold? And would the child have been as lost if it was summer or spring or autumn, or was that child more lost *because* it was winter?)

I don't know.

All Dickens says in A Christmas Carol is that *bye and bye they had a song, about a lost child travelling in the snow, from Tiny Tim; who had a plaintive little voice, and sang it very well indeed.*

So how about I tell you instead some more verifiable kinds of thing –

(what's verifiable?)

Verifiable means things we can prove are true because of facts that exist in the world about them –

(okay)

– for instance, I could tell you a very verifiable fact or two –

(very very fiable, ha ha!)

– about a man called Mr Kepler, who studied time and harmony and believed that truth and time were kindred –

(what's kindred?)

Kindred means family, what I'm saying is he thought that truth and time are sort of related, family to each other.

(Oh.)

He was one of the people who first identified Halley's comet, one of the first to realize it wasn't a different comet every time, which is what people had believed over the centuries, but was actually the same comet coming back to visit us again and again. And he was a man who paid things attention up close as well as far away. One day a single snowflake landed on the collar of his coat and he became one of the first people in history to count the sides of a piece of snow and write about how there's a repeating pattern in snow crystals.

(Is a snow crystal the same as a snowflake?)

It can be. But snowflake can also mean the thing that happens when two or more snow crystals fall together and create one structure all together. Anyway, he found there was a symmetry in the shapes of –

(what's symmetry again?)

it's, oh God, –

(it's God?)

No, ha ha, it's not God. But it'd be a nice idea of God, and I wish that *was* what God means. Symmetry means that things have a very similar shape, or reflect each other or match each other in a balanced way, or in harmony, it can also mean harmony. Your ears. They're symmetrical, and your eyes, your hands. But the thing Mr Kepler wondered was this. If every snow crystal had something in common with all the others but at the same time was still completely unique, different from any other snow crystal, what would be God's reason for making them like that? Because we're talking about the days when people thought such things mattered for metaphysical reasons –

(what's m–)

Oh Christ. Okay. Well. Meta means something changing, or going beyond itself, and physical means physical and anyway at least Mr Kepler never got lost or died in the snow, though Mr Descartes, who was a French philosopher and another snow lover, was so interested in snow that he went to live in a snowy country, Norway, or Denmark, or Finland or Sweden, and he was out in the cold so much that he caught pneumonia and died almost as soon as he moved there.

(Yeah, but what's metaph–)

– and then there's the farmer whose name I can't remember but who lived in America hundreds of years later and who loved snowflakes so much that he invented a camera with a microscope actually inside it, imagine –

(wow –)

– to take close-up photos of individual snow crystals. And he was out walking in a blizzard one day and *he* died *too* –

(oh no –)

So. What about that lost child, then? Lost in snow so heavy, so laden on the branches of the trees above but so glistening in what moonlight manages to break through the less thick places, that the snow forms a cold but moonlit and protective carapace from one end of the wood to the other, which leads straight to the gates of the underworld.

(What's carapace?)

It's a caravan that goes at a great pace.

(Is it?)

Ha ha! you believed me! No, really it's the word for, like, a shell, like the one a tortoise or a crab has on its back, the hard thing that protects their soft insides from the outside world. It's also a word for something that covers you over and protects you.

(Like armour?)

Exactly. And the underworld, you know what the underworld is, don't you?

(Yes.)

What is it, then?

(It's a world underneath a world.)

Well, people tend to think of the underworld as the opposite of heaven, in other words as a hell, a place of brimstone, rocks that turn molten and melt into each other like the stuff that can sometimes in history cover Italian towns like Pompeii and Herculaneum and preserve them for centuries when it explodes out of volcanoes. But no. Because the underworld is the opposite of hot. Like winter's the opposite of summer. It's a place where everything and everyone is dead and cold and dark, a bit like being – imagine, imagine this – inside a crow-plucked empty eyesocket –

(uch)

– but if that eyesocket was as big as a huge underground cave, bigger than any of the London train stations, say –

(wow, okay)

– and the interesting thing, since we're talking about extreme heat and extreme cold, is that both heat and cold can both hurt *and* preserve, in different ways. Like when the great philosopher Mr Bacon, who also by the way died of the cold, caught a chill by hanging about outside in freezing weather filling the insides of a dead chicken with snow to see if keeping meat frozen might mean human beings could store it for longer. Anyway. Where were we?

(Carapace.)

Yes. The child walks all the way through the woods under the carapace of snow until it comes to the gates of the underworld. There's a huge door made of ice, and it's so tall that the child looking up can't see where the door ends. But the child knocks at the door with all the confidence of a child lost in the snow at midwinter expecting help, warmth and comfort, and it can do this, the child, are you listening? –

(yes –)

it can do this *because* it's midwinter, which is a time of year when children and gods are meant to meet, when a child can speak to gods and gods are meant to listen, a time that's about children and gods being related.

(Family.)

The child knocks on the door, a door so cold that the child's fist sticks to its surface with each knock and the child has to tear it off nearly ripping the skin on its hand, and it's hard to tell whether anybody's heard the knock because if you knock on ice the sound just disappears.

But then there's a sudden terrible deafening noise. The child looks up and sees, shaking in the sky, a hundred giant door keys made of carved ice.

Go away, a voice made of ice says.

Can you tell the landlord or landlady of this place that I've been lost in the snow for ages, the child says.

Come back when you're dead, the ice voice says.

And can you ask him or her to find me a warm corner to rest in, the child says, and something to eat and drink, just till I get my bearings?

The ice door sighs a sigh as big as a hurricane. Then something picks up that child, swings it up into the air by the shoulders of its coat using icy fingers that are layered with teeth, like shark teeth, which pierce right through the wool of the coat and graze and burn the skin all round the child's neck. Then it drags the child down through a freezing dark labyrinth at the speed of death.

(Oh.)

But don't worry. Because the child shoots through that underworld like hot blood through the veins of every cold dead person who grew up to be lost in the snow, and there are *millions* of them, and the child passes like warm blood through them all and what the child is seeing when it does is pure colour, the colour green, Christmas green, green at its brightest, because green isn't just a summer colour after all, no, green's truly a winter colour too.

(Is it?)

The earth is made of it. Green. Moss, algae, lichen, mould. It's the colour everything was before there were flowers, the colour of the first trees, the trees that didn't have leaves, had needles instead, the trees that grew in the first hiatus between cold and warm –

(what's hiatus?)

Hiatus is the word for a short pause. And Christmas trees are related to those first original green trees, and they grew even before the world decided to invent all the other colours. It's the green of the holly that made the red of the berry.

(Trees have families?)

They do. And God knows where the child in this story got this following bit of trivia but as you know it's verifiably true that the colour green also happens to be one of the easiest colours to erase when people are having their photos taken or film taken of them, because putting an image against a blue or green background will make it easier to cut round them or to blend them later to make it look like they're somewhere they aren't, on a flying carpet, say, or simply floating in space like an astronaut.

(Yes.)

This is what the child's thinking about before those iceblade fingers slacken their grip and let that child drop in a heap on to a floor as cold as a butcher's slab, and –

(what's a butcher's slab?)

I'll tell you later. Remind me. But imagine the

child for me, now, thin as a blade of grass before the great god of the underworld, towering above on his throne of ice, a god each of whose hands alone is like a massive automated shop-display of flick knives made of ice.

(Oh.)

The child stands up, straightens the coat, brushes it down, feels for where the ice-teeth went through the wool with an annoyed tch at the rows of holes.

Then the god speaks.

Still alive? the god says.

The child breathes out through its nose so its breath is visible in the cold. Then it makes a face at the god as if to say, see?

Well well, the god says. A survivor.

Chilly in here, the child says.

You call this chilly? the god says. I'm the god of cold. This is nothing. I'll show you chilly. And stop doing that.

Doing what? the child says.

The god is pointing at the child's feet.

The child looks down too. Its feet have disappeared. It is ankle-deep in water. The child is melting through the floor.

As each second passes, the floor round the child thaws a little more.

Stop it, I said, the god says.

The child shrugs.

How? the child says.

The god begins to panic. He loses his grip on his own slippery throne. He flails around on it at the head of the great hall of ice.

Stop that right now, the god shouts.

In the middle of the night the village church bell rang midnight.

Again?

But midnight was already well past. Wasn't it?

Sophia got up. She went downstairs.

The young woman Arthur had brought with him was sitting at the kitchen table. She was halfway through a plate of scrambled eggs.

Would you like some? the woman said.

She said it quietly as if not to wake anybody though nobody was asleep anywhere near the kitchen.

Sophia said nothing. She stood in the doorway and looked towards the sink where there was an unwashed pan on the side.

The young woman followed the direction of the look and leapt to her feet.

I'll do it right now, she said.

She did; she washed the pan, again with a degree of care and quietness. Then she put it back in the right place without having to be told where.

Sophia nodded.

She turned in the doorway and went back to bed.

She settled down under the covers.

The head settled back on her shoulder.

Earlier, as Christmas Eve had turned into Christmas Day, she had listened at the window to the faraway church bell from the village ringing midnight. It was a still night and not cold, the wind in the direction to send the sound of the bell here; it would be a warm start to Christmas after the storms, and the lack of frost and cold left the landscape wintry without dignity; the bell's resonance was more pedestrian than it'd have been on the kind of crisp cold winter night tonight ideally ought to have been. Dead. Dead. Dead, the bell went. Or maybe: Head. Head. Head. The village church had only one bell so couldn't play a tune. It sounded, she thought, like someone at the back of memory hitting at stone with an axe, which is an act that'll do nothing but ruin a good blade.

But the head, merry in the threshold of the open window, had played a game of inside/outside with itself to the steady toll of the bell.

The head had lost some of its hair since yesterday. It looked bedraggled. But it smiled serenely, cheshire catly, and closed its eyes in pleasure at the place where the outside air met the warm in the room, swinging like a pendulum, bracing itself against the wind direction when the wind blew, perching on her wrist like an obedient bird of prey when she closed the window, then allowing itself to be deposited on the bed on the pillow next to her own.

To get the head to go to sleep she'd told it the Christmas story.

A woman is visited by an angel. Then the woman is about to give birth. A man who isn't the father of the child the woman is having but is a very nice man and an integral father-figure part of the Family is leading the donkey with the woman on its back for miles and miles to a town that's full of people because a ruler has ordered a people count. No room at the inn. No room at the inn. No room at the inn and the baby coming.

An innkeeper offers the couple a place to have the baby where he usually keeps his livestock. Oh, the star, she'd forgotten about the star. It's how the people know to come and visit the child in the manger, infant of Mary, and she started to sing that song to it but it was too out of her range so she sang the little donkey song instead.

Then she told the head about Nina and Frederik, the duo who originally sang the donkey song. They were foreign, rather glamorous, she said, I think one of them was an aristocrat from Austria or Scandinavia. It was quite a hit-parade hit at the time.

The head had listened with the same grave attentive face to the story of the birth, the story of the donkey and the names of the foreign pop stars. It had rolled gently back and fore on the pillow as she sang about the bells ringing out the word Bethlehem.

Then it had given her a singular thank-you glance, after which it removed, as if by magic, all expression whatsoever from itself, dimmed into a colourless statue like the blank-eyed face of an ancient stone Roman.

More of its hair had come loose on the pillow in a semicircle round it. She'd gathered up the hair and put it in its substantial clumps on the bedside table. The newly visible top of the head's head, which the hair had covered till now, was very pale, fragile looking as a child's fontanelle. So she'd got up and found a large handkerchief at the back of the handkerchief drawer. She wrapped it round the top of the head in case the head was cold without its hair. She got back into bed and put the bedside light out. The near-bald head had smiled at her and glowed in the dark in its new turban as if lit by Rembrandt, as if Rembrandt had painted the child Simone de Beauvoir.

She lay in bed now feeling the weight of the sleeping head and thinking about how she'd probably be physically sick if she were ever to eat anything again as rich as scrambled eggs, especially cooked in butter like the woman had made them.

Though it might be worth it, to re-experience what it's like to be sick, because from what she remembered there was a certain pleasure in it, anarchic force of clearance, one of those powerful liminal times in a life when death isn't just preferable to being alive, because you feel so lousy, but that also let you negotiate with the powers that be about your own living or dying.

She drifted between sleep and wake holding the head in her arms and dream-dozing of an array of necks with no heads, headless stone torsos, headless Madonnas, baby Jesuses with missing heads or just necks or half-heads. Then the chipped-headless saints in reliefs came into her head, and the ones carved on the fonts and so on, the knocked-off nothing-but-necks in Reformation-vandalized churches in whatever self-righteousness of fury, whatever intolerant ideology of the day. There was always a furious intolerance at work in the world no matter when or where in history, she thought, and it always went for the head or the face. She thought of the burnt-off scraped-off faces of the medieval painted saints on the wooden altar screens in hundreds of churches like the one whose bell across the fields had been ringing in this year's Christmas, dead,

head,

which were perhaps more beautiful *for* the damage done them, the rich reds and golds of the fleur-de-lis backdrops, the richly painted fabrics of the flowing clothes below the space where the head or the face should be, the vividly detailed artefacts they carried to show you which saint or apostle each figure was meant to represent (a chalice, a cross, a different shaped cross, a book, a knife, a sword, a key) because the people who wanted to destroy them never went for the artefact, or the heart. Under the golden halos where the faces should be – like masks, but also paradoxically like all masks had been lifted – there'd be burnt blackened wood.

It was meant as a warning. *Take a look at what your saints are truly made of.* It was the demonstration that everything symbolic will be revealed as a lie, everything you revere nothing but burnt matter, broken stone, as soon as it meets whatever shape time's contemporary cudgel takes.

But it worked the other way round too. They looked, those vandalized saints and statues, more like statements of survival than of destruction. They were proof of a new state of endurance, mysterious, headless, faceless, anonymous.

The sleeping head on Sophia's shoulder grew heavy.

She looked down at it, her very own Christmas infant, because it looked infant-like now that its hair was missing, as if returning to baby state. It was sleeping, yes, like a baby (though nothing like the infant Arthur, who'd been a squalling appalling dark night of the soul. Perhaps she'd have been a different person if her own child had been a bit more like this; perhaps Arthur would, too). An eyelash fell off on to its cheek, then another, and between just the fall of each tiny lash the infant planet grew heavier, markedly so, pressing against her shoulderbone quite painfully, though not heavily enough to pin her down because she sat up very suddenly (and the head, still fast asleep, rolled off like a hardboiled Easter egg over her arm down her side and into a dip in the bed along her thigh) at what she thought next:

Where had that young woman Arthur had brought here got the eggs she was cooking earlier?

There *were* no eggs in the fridge.

There *was* no butter.

Well, there was one egg. She'd bought six, but more than two months ago.

If that woman had eaten that egg she'd be dying, and painfully, and soon, of food poisoning.

Could food poisoning make you fall unconscious?

Because what if the young woman was lying on

the floor unconscious in a pool of her own disgorgement down in the kitchen?

The bell rang midnight from the village church.

Again?

Oh come *on*.

Sophia got up. She went downstairs.

The woman in the kitchen wasn't dead or unconscious. She was fine. She looked up when Sophia opened the door.

Oh hi, she said.

Are you unwell at all? Sophia said.

Unwell? she said. No. I'm very well thank you. I'm feeling pretty good, better than usual.

Is this my second time coming downstairs, or is it my first? Sophia said.

It's your second, the woman said.

And you're Charlotte, Sophia said.

I'm Charlotte here for this Christmas weekend, the woman said.

What is your surname, Charlotte? Sophia said.

Um, the woman said.

She looked blankly at Sophia for a moment. Then she said:

Bain.

A Scottish name, Sophia said.

If you say so, Charlotte Bain said.

But you're not Scottish. Where are you from originally? Sophia said.

Charlotte Bain laughed a little laugh.

Try to guess, she said. If you guess right I'll give you – let's make it worth the bet. I'll give you a thousand pounds.

I never gamble, Sophia said.

You are a very wise woman, Charlotte Bain said.

You're not English, I know that, I can hear it in your voice, Sophia said. My own father inherited an abiding hatred of people from particular other countries, from his time in the war.

Which war is that? Charlotte Bain said.

Don't be obtuse, Sophia said. *The* war. The Second World War. It accented his life. If anyone came on television or on the radio speaking a language or a particularly accented English, or if anyone from somewhere he abhorred came into a room he happened to be in, he'd leave the room. He hated Germans. He hated the French for collaborating. Even hearing a certain singer sing was enough to reduce him to rage. Then, in his life after the war, he worked in finance. This gave him a range of more illogical but just as heady hatreds of particular races and ethnicities. But I myself am from a more open-minded generation and will accept you, since you are Arthur's partner, as every bit as English as myself.

Thanks, Charlotte Bain said. But I'm not. English.

You are to me, Sophia said (and put her hand in

the air to stop further remonstration). Now. Tell me. How did you meet my son?

I'm sure your son's already bored you with that story, Charlotte Bain said.

I'm asking *you* to bore me with it, Sophia said.

Oh. Well. Okay. I will. I met him at a bus stop, Charlotte Bain said. I was at a bus stop on my day off and he came up and started talking to me. We went for a coffee. He bought me something to eat.

And you've known each other how long? Sophia said.

It still feels pretty new to me, Charlotte Bain said. Couple of days.

Are you in this kitchen and not asleep in a bed because I told you you'd have to sleep in the barn? Sophia said. Because if so, I renege on my earlier dictat. You are welcome to sleep in the house.

Not at all, Charlotte Bain said. I'm not that tired, I had a sleep on the train on the way here. Plus we waited up to let your sister in and we made up some beds, I hope it's all right, I found the linen in the cupboard in the upstairs hall. And then I thought I should maybe eat something and after that I was just awake anyway, it gets past the point when I can fall asleep and it's been lovely and warm in here with that big cooker and there was a bird singing, I could hear it through that window, so I just sat and listened and I kind of forgot about it.

You what? My what? Sophia said.

Sleeping. I forgot about sleeping, Charlotte
Bain said.

You waited up to let in whom? Sophia said.

Your sister, Charlotte Bain said.

In this house? Sophia said.

Yes, Charlotte Bain said.

Here? Now? Sophia said.

She was tired, Charlotte Bain said. She got here
about a quarter to three, long drive from wherever,
and she went off to bed and we put away the stuff
and then your son went to bed too.

Stuff, Sophia said.

Charlotte Bain crossed the room and opened the
door of the fridge.

Like a fridge in someone else's house, or in an
advert, or a film about ideal everyday family life, it
was full of food. The brightness, freshness and
cram of it were shocking.

Christ, Sophia said. The last thing I need.

Sophia, back in bed with the head beside her, heard
the village church bell toll twelve.

Again.

Sophia sighed.

Unless it was another Christmas Day altogether
right now. Which it is, Christmas Day 1977, a
Sunday, but it being Christmas Day seems to make
no difference at all to the people in this big

falling-apart old house in Cornwall in which her sister Iris is now – you can't call it living, since Iris and this bunch of foreigners and layabouts here are paying no rent to anyone – squatting, there's no other word for it and her sister Iris is far too old to be living like a student, she'll be forty in three years' time.

Her sister Iris is making nothing of her life. Sophia thinks of their mother, when Iris worked at the filling station, telling anyone who asked how her daughters were doing that Iris had a good position in an oil company.

And it's Christmas but it's not like Christmas in any way. Their mother'd have abhorred that too. It could be just another Sunday, any old Sunday. No, it doesn't even have the atmosphere special to a Sunday. It could be any day of the week, a Monday, Tuesday, Wednesday.

No. It doesn't even have *that*. More like *no* day.

The only way you'd know, the only clue you'd have that it's Christmas or any special kind of day, if aliens from other planets for example really existed and you were an alien and had landed your spaceship in the (surprisingly sizeable) grounds round this (clearly once really lovely, what you call rambling, presumably old money) property in its (middle of nowhere) rural location, is the TV set being on and the more-Christmassy-than-usual revolving world going round on the BBC, plus the

116

fact that National Velvet is on TV right now
though it's nearly lunchtime.

Not that it looks like there's going to be anything
resembling Christmas lunch served up here.
Christmas is probably too bourgeois. Plus, two of
the (God knows how many, it feels like fifty but it is
truthfully closer to fifteen) dropouts Iris now lives
with are asleep in here, one on each old couch, and
it's possible they've been here since last night, all
night, haven't gone to bed or taken clothes off or
anything that normal people do, instead just fell
asleep where they were and haven't yet woken.

So even if Sophia had wanted to sit in here and
watch a comforting old classic like this on
Christmas morning, this Christmas above all when
her father is in fucking New Zealand and her
mother is fucking dead, there's nowhere to sit
except on this hard chair, the legs of which are
uneven.

Commune.

Squat. Mouse droppings, look, there, on the
floor.

Ethical alternative anarchic living.

Weak excuse for living irresponsibly. Illegal dirty
hippy-hangover pseudo-romantic squat. But
someone here is clever enough at least to have made
its generator work, so there's electricity, for which
relief much thanks (Hamlet), because it's bitter cold
and Sophia is feeling pretty sick at heart. One of the

117

men living here, though, she thinks his name is
Paul, has a very interesting looking Chinese dark
striped cotton padded jacket. Iris, whose
housemates all call her Ire, saw her yesterday
picking the jacket up off one of the tables they pile
their coats up on in the house's decrepit orangerie
and turning it inside out to look at the seams to see
if there was a label, which there wasn't.

Think you've just given my whizz kid sister her
inspiration for next year's market, Paul, Iris said
and put her arm round Sophia.

This is Soph, she said through the cigarette
smoke to the roomful of people when Sophia
arrived. Which room would you like, Soph?

The house apparently has sixteen bedrooms
though some of them have holes in their ceilings
and one is lived in by birds who come through a
hole in the rooftiles and are roosting in the room
for the winter, and the people who live here don't
have a room per se, they just take whichever one
they feel like sleeping in on the night.

Not the one with the hole in the roof thank you,
Sophia had said and everybody in the room had
laughed. The kitchen was full of people; someone
moved up on the bench at the table so she could sit
down and join in the conversation.

They were talking about a place in Italy where a
farmer had one day been working in his farmyard
and had seen his cat just fall over on to its side.

When he went to see what it was doing, he found it was dead. He picked it up. Its tail fell off.

Sophia laughed. A laugh just burst out of her, it couldn't not, at the thought of the cat and its tail falling off.

Nobody else laughed. Everybody turned and looked at her. She stopped laughing.

The cat had died because last year a valve had blown in a factory near this farm, and the chemicals the factory was making had leaked out in a cloud, and because the area was a place known for its furniture-making the disaster was still happening all these months later because nobody in the world now wanted to buy any furniture made in that place in case the wood was poisonous. Nobody there had even really known there was a leak till all the leaves had fallen off the place's trees, dead like winter though it was July, and its birds had fallen dead out of the sky, and cats and rabbits and other small creatures had keeled over dead. Then the people who lived locally started taking their children to the hospital because their faces had broken out in rashes and boils. But the factory owners still hadn't reported the leak to anyone in authority. So it wasn't till after a few weeks of the poison being in the air that the authorities sent in the army to evacuate one of the towns the leak had affected, and the people who lived there had had to leave everything they owned in their houses, which must have been terrible because their houses were then bulldozed and buried under a massive mound of earth and people were warned not to eat the salad or the fruit grown locally. Now nobody living there knew whether they were ill or not and a lot of farmstock was being destroyed and people who lived locally had been told by the authorities not to try to have children.

Sophia's mind wandered.

She looked up at the consonants and vowels of what looked like a nonsense Scrabble game the people living here had painted round the room's cornicing, still quite elegant regardless of the disrepair. i s o p r o p y l m e t h y l p h o s p h o f l u o r i d a t e w i t h d e a t h.

Those were actually words, or almost words.

I. So. Prop. Me. Meth. Ethyl. Wasn't it more usually Ethel? And that was almost the word fluoride. Definitely date, and with, and death, there at the end.

One of the people at the table was talking now about how she'd heard from a friend of a friend of hers that someone she knew from the place where the disaster had happened had gone on holiday to another place in Italy and the people who owned the hotel had told them not to mention where they were from in case everyone else staying in the hotel panicked and left.

The girl next to Sophia passed her a couple of

120

creased bits of paper with photographs on them. Two cats were lying on their sides in a grassy field like they were asleep. They didn't look dead, they looked normal, like cats but weird, lying flat on their sides with their eyes shut. There was a child's face with a blistered texture like sandpaper: the child was smiling because she was having her photograph taken.

It was terrible what could happen in other countries, Sophia said and everybody round the table fell about laughing as if she'd made a very funny joke.

Then they'd started discussing, for her benefit, a place that sounded as if it was just up the road with a name that sounded like someone in music hall or Dickens. A secret factory there made CBWs, they said. They said things in acronyms all the time; the women draped themselves over the men and the men talked in capital letters. It made CBWs. It made OPs. It made something that sounded like TCP.

Well, TCP is really useful, Sophia said. You can pretty much use it on anything.

Someone laughed at that, just one person, a man called Mark. Someone else, one of the girls, she had a once-nice woollen jumper on though now unravelling at the side, leaned over, offered Sophia a cigarette and asked what she did for a living.

My sister's a woman of import, Iris said standing

behind Sophia and tousling her hair like she's a child. Left school, started a business while she was still studying at college, she was only in her first year and she made a fistful of money out of Afghan coats. Probably more than a couple of you in this room bought one of my genius sister's coats. What's the latest seller, Soph?

Macramé, Sophia said. In bags and bikinis, and clothes too. Greece has really opened up in the last couple of years. And djellabas are still selling, and the latest thing is a new kind of polyester, cheap but really hard-wearing, feels more natural, it actually really does, and the people in the know are sure it's going to do well in the gap left by cheesecloth.

Silence round the table.

Broderie anglaise is still popular too, of course, Sophia said. Being, I think, quite timeless, and yet also good when worn ironically as part of the punk style.

More silence.

Then the man who is clearly Iris's current partner, whose name is Bob, started talking about people in their area who had worked for the military and were now suffering from illnesses and everybody had stopped looking at Sophia in the silent judgement way and looked engaged in world politics again instead.

The wallpaper in this room with the TV in it looks original. Turn of the century? What a lovely house it could be if it were somebody's actual house. Sophia, sitting on the hard chair watching Elizabeth Taylor walk along a track in the kind of brilliant technicolor that only really makes sense at Christmas, the kind you know is still technicolor even when you're watching it on a black and white set like this one, wonders now how Iris feels about seeing that word death on the kitchen wall every day, every time she makes a cup of tea or just walks through the kitchen. Iris didn't come home for the funeral. Couldn't bear to? Wasn't allowed to? Just couldn't be bothered to?

There is no mentioning Iris's name at home.

She'd listened last night to one of the people here rather formally closing the conversation as if it had been some kind of a meeting rather than people just hanging out together round a table, by reading out loud to everyone from what they said was a classic book about spring; the woman, Gail, read a story that sounded at first like a Christmas story but clearly wasn't one. *In the gutters under the eaves and between the shingles of the roofs, a white granular powder still showed a few patches; some weeks before it had fallen like snow upon the roofs and the lawns, the fields and streams. No witchcraft, no enemy action had silenced the rebirth of new life in this stricken world. The people had done it themselves.*

It was all so symbolic and heavy.

She'd gone up to her freezing room on the top floor of this house, arctic after the fires downstairs; she'd been trying to warm herself under her coat when Iris had knocked on the door of it, she'd brought an electric fire up.

Knew you'd be feeling the cold, she said.

She plugged it in. Sophia pulled the edge of the coat over the Radio Times she'd brought with her. One of the things she'd most liked about Christmas at home, at least in the time since Iris stopped coming home for Christmas, was going through her parents' Christmas double issue and marking with a pen a little cross next to the things she planned to pass the time watching. She'd been reading it, near tears, before Iris came to the door of the room on what will have been the servants' floor, dilapidated, whose carpeting was ancient, whose flooring, where there was no carpet and no lino or lining, was paintstained rough wood. The Radio Times this year has a front cover with what looks from a distance like a jolly Christmas tree on it, and then when you get closer the tree turns into a lovely snowy typically English village with a path through the middle of it, a dog at a gate, a postbox, and she covered it with her coat to hide it when Iris sat on the edge of the old mattress to show her a pile of her mail that had arrived ripped open and held together with Post Office sticky tape. *Found open or damaged and officially sealed.* For some reason

Iris found the sticky tape funny. Then she kissed Sophia on the head and went back downstairs to her friends.

She didn't mention, she hadn't yet mentioned, their mother.

Now Sophia is passing Christmas Day in a room with a couple of sleeping people she doesn't know watching Velvet Brown's mother, harsh but loving, make it possible for her daughter to ride in the Grand National.

That red postbox on the front of the Radio Times: why does it mean so much and at the same time so little? She wants it to mean again like meaning used to mean. And why is this a day that had a meaning before but even while it carries on having that meaning, meaning so much to so many people, why can't it have that meaning any more here and now for her? The very notion of the name of a day of the week having to have a meaning makes her feel tired at a level she's never known tiredness could go to.

There is a new meanness in meaning.

Deep breath, Sophia.

In a little while, it'll be Billy Smart's Circus. Then the big afternoon film today is The Wizard of Oz.

Well, The Wizard of Oz is partly in black and white anyway.

The big film season on the BBC this year is a series of Elvis movies. Elvis is dead too, now.

When Iris comes into the TV room bringing her a mug of something hot, not tea or coffee but something that smells of farmyards, Sophia says:

Do you remember the day you got me out of school to see G.I. Blues and we went to London?

Iris is still half asleep. Her hair is all up on one side of her head, it needs brushing or a wash. She smells even more of this house than this house does. She smells fuggy, of sex. Everyone in the house does. She leans on the back of the old sofa and yawns without covering her mouth as the Grand National people unbutton the clothes on the knocked-unconscious child Elizabeth Taylor.

Nope, she says.

She rubs at her face with both hands.

They're showing them all on TV this Christmas now he's dead, all the movies, Sophia says.

It takes a death sometimes to make us all live a bit more, Iris says.

Platitude, cliché, Sophia thinks. She feels like a cowed child. She has felt more and more childlike and cowed since she arrived here. Nevertheless, she perseveres.

It was on the BBC yesterday morning, she says. G.I. Blues.

Uh huh, Iris says.

You let me wear your jacket. We went for coffee. You took me to the 2i's, Sophia says.

126

Iris heaves herself up off the back of the sofa and yawns again.

A million wild horses wouldn't have dragged me to see a film with Elvis playing stupid war games in it, she says as she leaves the room.

She turns and winks at Sophia as she goes.

Dead.

Head.

Head.

Dead.

Twelve.

Midnight again, for Christ sake. The church bell rang it for the fifth time that night. Sophia made an exasperated sound. She turned over in her bed.

The head lay next to her. It didn't move. It was as still as a stone.

It was a prank, surely a prank, a renegade village child out swinging on the rope of that bell to make people who heard it think they were going mad.

Then it's a summer and Arthur aged ten comes through from the front of the house into the office where Sophia has to be because she hasn't a choice and has to work from home almost the whole time Arthur's home for the holidays.

It's from the mid-1990s, this memory, if Arthur is ten years old in it.

Mum, there's a woman on the news who looks really familiar, Arthur says.

I'm working, Sophia says.

I really recognize her but I can't think who she is, Arthur says.

And? Sophia says.

I thought if you see her too you might, he says.

Is this some kind of game to make me come through and watch TV with you? Sophia says.

No, I just want you to look at this one thing, Arthur says. This one person. For one minute. It won't even take as much as a minute. Some seconds only. Ten at the most. And if you don't hurry she won't be on it any more.

Sophia sighs. She writes something down, memorizes where she is on the spreadsheet, leaves the cursor next to the figure she's got to on the screen and gets up from the computer.

When she comes into the front room Iris is on the TV. She is holding forth. What she's talking about is sheep dip.

In the drinking water, Iris says. Crop spraying. Relation of pesticides to nerve gas. Relation of nerve gas to Nazis.

Iris looks a lot older. She has put on weight. She has let herself go grey.

She is on the whole weathering rather badly. Depression, anxiety, confusion, she is saying. People placed in mental hospitals, of course, because medical system ignorance leads to misdiagnosis. No recognition of the wide range of symptoms. Difficulty in using language. Hallucination. Headaches. Joint pains.

She is being filmed in a sunny field somewhere, the grass bleached and the trees, full-crowned and dusty with summer, moving in the wind in the distance behind her.

This industry is the offspring, the child if you like, of the Second World War, she is saying.

The camera cuts to the interviewer nodding then back to Iris's face. Past her face, past the screen, behind the news footage on the TV, here on the edge of Hampstead through the patio doors the early evening is gorgeous too, sunny like it'll never not be sunny again, and the people next door are having a barbecue in their garden, their children squealing with happiness and jumping in and out of a paddling pool. The programme returns to the news studio. An expert in the studio tells the newsreader that everything that Iris said is laughable and untrue.

We all mine and undermine and landmine ourselves, in our own ways, in our own time, Sophia thinks.

What are you doing watching TV inside on a day like this? she says out loud. Haven't you anywhere more interesting to be or anything more interesting to do?

Arthur, kneeling in front of the TV, turns round. He looks crushed. Sophia has to work very hard – it is very, very hard – not to be hurt in the heart every time by every single one of her son's vulnerabilities.

I thought I knew her, he says. Do we know her?

No, Sophia says. That was nobody we know.

She goes back through to the office and puts her finger on the number she'd written down.

She looks at the figures on the screen again.

Yes. Good.

Midnight again.

Sophia counted the chimes.

The umpteenth midnight of the night, she told the head. The head didn't care. The head was the kind of silent they say graves are.

She rolled the head into her hands on the coverlet and picked it up.

It was heavy, the heaviest it had yet felt.

It had no eyes now.

It had no mouth.

Well, but perhaps that was a good thing. Let's think of it as a good thing.

But there's face, and there's faceless. Neither's always so simply a good thing. For instance, one November evening (what year is it now? sometime in the early 80s, going by her clothes) either Sophia loses her balance, or a nice-enough seeming chap, someone she's never met before, nudges her in the small of her back so that she falls down half the

130

flight of stairs between the floors in the block in which her flat's on the second floor.

Some days before this happens, this other thing also happens. A quite different man, a man driving an open-topped car, which is strange because the weather isn't in any way conducive to taking the roof down on a convertible, draws up beside her as she locks her own car in a car park not far from a retailer to whom she's paying a visit and this man asks her if she'll mind getting in beside him for a moment to discuss a pressing matter.

She walks right past him. She doesn't even give him a second glance.

But the man is suddenly there again driving at a crawl next to her out in the open street. His car has its top closed now in the drizzle but its passenger window is wound right down and the man calls across to Sophia from the driver's seat that what he wants to discuss with her is important, a matter of life and death, and asks again if she won't mind just stepping into the car and having a quiet word with him.

She keeps walking as if he's not there. She looks straight ahead. She turns and walks into the department store she happens to be passing.

She hides behind the door she's just gone through.

She stands there close to one of the perfume counters and waits in the high mix of scents, watching the door, every so often checking behind her and all round her.

When she gets to the office she calls the police and reports the man and the registration number on his MG.

That was some days ago. Tonight when she gets home to her flat its front door is wide open.

There is no way on earth she left her front door open like that this morning.

A man she doesn't know is in her house. She can see him through the open door. He is sitting at the table in the dining room. He gives her a smile and a little wave hello as if they're friends. But they aren't.

Who the bloody hell are you? she says from the door.

Welcome home. Come in, he says.

How did you? she says.

The man holds both his hands up empty, as if in surrender. He pats the chair next to him.

She stays by the open front door. He gestures to the chair next to him again.

You may as well, he says. I just need a few minutes of your time. Moments, that's all. Just the time it takes to show you these.

She comes through into the dining room and stands well back from the table. It is covered in photographs and photocopies. They seem to be of people who're still alive but who've been shot or hurt. One man is bleeding all down his legs.

Another man has been shot in what was once his face.

Then he shows her a photograph of what looks like a black cave of a room. She sees a hand connected to nothing in the foreground, just lying on the floor like a glove, and then, under a table by itself, a shape that looks like it might be a head.

I'll be honest. We need your help, he says. We know already what kind of a person you are in the world. We'd like ourselves and others all across the country, all across the world, to benefit from what we know to be your very good sense.

He tells her that a trusted system of monitoring persons of interest is one of the ways of avoiding atrocities like the ones in the photographs.

Persons of what? she says. Monitoring what?

He tells her that monitoring generally helps to keep things clean and neat.

He suggests that he knows she knows there is such a thing as truth, and that the gentle monitoring of those close to us who may or may not be charting anywhere on a fairly wide scale from person of interest to radical activist can sometimes be crucial in disproving their involvement in certain circumstances.

In other words can sometimes quite redeem them too, he says.

Redeem, she says.

A very good word, the man says.

You do know I'm no longer a Roman Catholic? she says.

He gives her a disarming smile and nods warmly, as if he approves of everything she's ever done.

He really does seem like a very nice man indeed.

Whoever you are, she says, I'd like you to leave my house right now.

Flat, he says. The correct term for this place is flat. Apartment, if we were over the pond. It's nice, though. Cosy.

He shuffles his photographs and papers together and takes a piece of card or paper out of his pocket. He puts it on the table.

For when you need to make contact, he says. Ask for Mr Barth. And think about it. Doesn't take much. We just need to know simple things. Whens, wheres, whos. Perfectly innocent. Because after all. The answer to life's mysteries.

Is what? she says.

I'm sorry? he says.

What's the answer, according to you, to life's mysteries? she says.

The answer is a question, the man says still sitting uninvited at her table. And the question is. Into whose myth do we choose to buy?

I'll show you out of the building, now, Mr Barth, she says.

Oh, *I'm* not Mr Barth, he says.

Is Mr Barth the man in the MG, then? she says.

I've absolutely no idea, he says.

Is he something to do with you too? she says.

I simply couldn't say, he says.

He shrugs back his chair and stands up. She leads the way back out through the open door and on to the staircase down to the first floor. When he pushes her, or when she lurches forward and loses her balance, or both, there are six or seven steps still to fall. As she lands she hurts her arm quite badly.

Oh God, he says. Do be careful.

He picks her up at the bottom of the flight. He holds her very steadily by the sore arm. He looks her in the eyes.

What a nasty fall, he says. I hope you're all right. What a thing to happen.

And you're a total bastard, she says. Come near me again and I'll.

You will, won't you, he says.

He smiles at her, what she can only call, afterwards in her head, an intelligent smile, one that understands how clever she is herself.

When she comes back upstairs to her flat, not house, she finds the card with the telephone number typed on it tucked under a corner of one of the place mats.

Christ.

She goes back to the closed front door and fixes the chain across it.

She closes the curtains in all four rooms. She pulls down the blind in the kitchenette even though all it looks on to is a brick wall.

Then she sees her own hand in the act of pulling the blind down and she snorts out a laugh.

She lets go, lets the blind flick back up again on its own.

She takes the chain off the front door on the way to the bathroom.

They can come in if they like.

She goes and gets that little card and tucks it behind the carriage clock on the mantelpiece.

She runs a bath.

Outside somewhere in the city, or town, or village, wherever she was, a bell was ringing, yes, again, midnight. Where was she now? Could you stop time? Could you stop time playing itself through you? Too late now, because here came Sophia in that bath she just ran more than thirty years ago soaping her sore arm and remembering as she does Iris and herself in their twin beds twenty years before that, a night when Iris was humouring her, helping her work out the harmony, Iris the high line, Soph the low, for the chorus of that song about Grocer Jack who didn't come back. Then Iris and Soph singing the harmonies they've made up themselves for the Elvis song she loves, singing the words in German, if their father's nowhere near and

136

if it's likely he'll overhear singing the translation
into English that Sophia made using the dictionaries
in the school library:

must I then
must I then
go and leave the little town
leave the little town
and you my dear stay here?

Iris: the kind of person who, if there's a sheepdog
in the room, say, and even though Iris is a stranger
in that room, in that house, even if she's never been
in that house before and met that dog, that
sheepdog will still come and bow before her with its
front legs stretched, then lie at her feet wherever she
sits and stay there all night with its nose on its
front paws.

Now here's the day when Sophia, home for the
weekend from college, decides she'll walk from the
station instead of take the bus, turns the corner into
their street and sees ahead of her a happening of
some sort outside her own home, a small crowd of
people watching Iris on the pavement, their father
standing square at the front gate, the front gate
closed, both his hands on its top bar. Their mother
is at the front door, half looking from the
doorframe. The suitcase on the ground at Iris's feet
is Sophia's suitcase. The suitcase is open on the
pavement. It has some clothes in it, bits and pieces
from Iris's room lying round about it on the

ground, like Iris is unpacking herself on to the street.

What's up? Sophia says.

Usual, Iris says. Can I borrow your case?

She puts the things on the pavement into the suitcase and heaves its two halves together. She clicks its locks, ties its straps, picks it up by its metal handle, swings it to feel the weight of it.

Where's she going? Sophia says to her father.

Sophia, their father says.

He says it in a way that means: do not involve yourself.

See you Philo, Iris says. I'll write.

Ever since Iris, who her parents keep saying is still not married, heard a thing on the radio about a gas place somewhere in England she's been like a one-person protest march about it, writing to the papers, putting up posters in the town square in the middle of the night, the police coming round because they've caught her painting over advertising hoardings on the sides of buildings with slogans in red paint, stuff about seals found dead on beaches nowhere near here *with their eyes burned out by something, Soph, and weals and burns all over them, imagine*, and the weapons being made in factories, again nowhere near here, miles and miles away, and making a scene in the front room every night till their father gets incandescent, about the harm done to the students' eyes in Paris and the people in Northern Ireland getting it fired at them too, *it's not harmless. It's poisonous. They call it an incapacitator, they say to the TV and newspaper people or the people who ask questions in parliament that it's just a smoke. Just a smoke. But it's related to the stuff they used in the trenches. Was that just a smoke? And on the people in the camps. Was that just a smoke?*

None of these things is happening here. They are all happening far away, elsewhere.

But they may as well be, Iris says. *What does here mean anyway, I'd like to know. Everywhere's a here, isn't it?*

Iris: a bloody liability. Trouble. Wasting her life. Warned and warned again. Reputation. Known to the authorities. Police record. Their father crying soundlessly into his supper. Their mother saying her usual downcast nothing, looking down at the nothing in her hands.

I'll write. I'll phone you at your college.

Iris walking down the street with the suitcase. All the neighbours watching her. Sophia watching her. Their father and mother watching her.

The neighbours only going back inside their houses when Iris has rounded the corner and gone.

Sophia is in the bath. A man has just pushed her downstairs and pretended not to.

To her knowledge Iris hasn't been up home since; Iris never saw their mother again; Iris hasn't seen their father either. Sophia has never known, and probably never will, what the straw was that broke the camel's back the night Iris left.

Straw. So light. *Just a smoke*.

Camel, broken back.

Such a violent piece of cliché.

Her arm hurts. There is going to be bruising all down her right side and thigh where she hit the railing and where her hip hit the edge of the bottom step; you don't have to fall very far, to hurt yourself considerably.

She sits on the side of the bath as it empties and towels herself dry with the good thick towels.

These towels are nothing like the thin things they had, that her father still has, still uses, up home.

Treat me right, treat me good,
treat me like you really should
cause I'm not made of wood
and I don't have a
wooden heart.

It was Christmas Day morning.

Thank God.

Thank the living daylight.

Sophia had sat at the edge of the bed, kept her excellent eyes open and dared midnight to catch her out. Oh midnight where's thy dinga-linga-ling. Midnight hadn't dared. Up came the light. Good old light. Good new light.

In fact the light had come up today marginally earlier than yesterday. And yesterday's light had been up a sliver earlier than the day's before that. There was this different quality to the light even only four days past the shortest day; the shift, the reversal, from increase of darkness to increase of light, revealed that a coming back of light was at the heart of midwinter equally as much as the waning of light.

Somewhere in this house right now her elder sister Iris was asleep.

Sophia sat at her dressing table and cradled the head in her arms.

The head wasn't really a head any more. It now had no face. It had no hair. It was as heavy as stone. It was smooth all over. Where its face had been was a surface like polished stone, worked, like marble.

It was hard to tell, now, which way up it ought to be, or which way round – things that had been obvious when the shape it took was a head.

It was now free of obviousness.

It now had a kind of self-symmetry.

She didn't really know what to call it now, head? stone? It was neither dead nor head. It was too heavy, too solid, to hover in the air any more or do those circus-trick spinning somersaults.

She put it on the table. She looked at it. She nodded.

But she felt for it. She didn't want it to grow cold.

She picked it up again, tucked it under her clothes on the skin of her abdomen and held it against her.

The round piece of stone the size of a small head lay there, did nothing. The nothing it did was intimate.

How could something be this uncomplicated?

How could it be, at the same time, so mysterious?

Look. It was nothing but a stone.

What a relief.

It was what the notion of relief aspired to and had always been meant to mean.

**Come with me now back to an early sunny
Saturday morning in September 1981,** to a piece of
English common land fenced off by the American
military in agreement with the British military,
where a car is pulling up across from the main gate
in the fence.

A woman gets out.

The woman comes straight over to the policeman
standing at the gate of the airbase in the high veil of
birdsong, the hum of the summer bees; there are
woods just over there.

The woman unfolds a piece of paper, holds it up
and begins to read from it. While she does, some
more women, one of them quite old, are running
across the neat cut grass towards the fence.

If this was a sitcom on the BBC the audience
would be laughing like anything.

You're early today, the policeman says to the woman.

The woman stops what she's reading. She looks at him. She looks down at the piece of paper and starts reading again from the top. He looks at his watch.

You're not due here till eight, he says.

The woman stops again. She points to the four women at the fence. She tells him they've chained themselves to it in an act of protest and that she's here to read him an open statement about this.

He is bewildered.

Are these women *not* the cleaners, then?

He looks across.

What have you done that for? he says.

Since they're not the cleaners he reports what's happening to the airbase on his radio.

The fence is made of wire mesh, millions of little wire-and-air diamonds and three rows of barbed wire on top, between a series of concrete posts in a circle nine miles long. The women have attached themselves to the main gate part of the fence by four little padlocks, the type people more usually use to padlock their suitcases. *All we could afford*.

A man in military uniform comes out of the base and talks with the policeman.

I thought they were the cleaners, the policeman says.

The first woman reads her letter to both of them.

This is some of what she reads out loud that morning:

We have undertaken this action because we believe that the nuclear arms race constitutes the greatest threat ever faced by the human race and our living planet. We in Europe will not accept the sacrificial role offered us by our North Atlantic Treaty Organization allies. We have had enough of our military and political leaders who squander vast sums of money and human resources on weapons of mass destruction while we can hear in our hearts the millions of human beings throughout the world whose needs cry out to be met. We are implacably opposed to the siting of Cruise Missiles in this country.

The women who've arrived here and chained themselves up with what's frankly such insubstantial ironware have been thinking overnight, they'll tell the historians afterwards, about what might happen to them for doing this. They haven't been able to get to sleep for thinking about guards and dogs, barking and shouting, and everything they can be charged for, from disturbing the peace all the way to treason. They expect at the least to be thrown in a cell, taken to court. A police record can mean the loss of your job.

They've eaten nothing and drunk very little for the last twelve hours. They're wearing clothes which will make reasonably discreet urinating possible. They're pretty sure the airbase authorities won't want them chained in such a prominent place for long.

They sit on the ground, settle back leaning against the fence as the woman reads the statement. The policeman and the military man stand there a bit bemused.

A little later in the morning the rest of the people who've been on the peace march arrive, and some new people who've joined in from the closest town; a lot of people who live in the town have wanted their common back for some time; it was requisitioned by the military decades ago when they spotted it from the air, ideal runway space.

A couple of reporters have turned up. The organizers tell them they're doing this as a protest to draw some substantial press attention to the march they're on and to get a bigger debate going in public about the missiles soon to be brought here. They say they're doing what the suffragettes knew to do.

One of them phones the Ministry of Defence and asks them about the women and the protest.

An official at the MOD tells the reporter that if it's true that some women have chained themselves to the fence, well, so what? The fence is on common land, land the MOD doesn't own. So this isn't the MOD's responsibility.

The official confirms that the MOD has no plans to move the women on.

Not a problem, the official says.

It all feels a bit anticlimactic.

Still, the weather is nice. Everybody sits on the neat mown grass in the sun as if they're all on an afternoon outing. Military people come and go, some taking photographs. A man arrives talking loudly about mug shots. He's the base commander. He addresses them. Afterwards, one of the women remembers how white the knuckles on his fists go while he does. He tells them, they say afterwards, that he'd like to machine-gun the lot of them. Then he tells them that as far as he's concerned they can stay there as long as they like. *Without his contemptuous dismissal, we wouldn't have stayed*, one of the protesters says years later. *I had five kids to get back to.*

When the afternoon is turning into evening another policeman comes over and suggests to the women that since it's Saturday night it might be best if they moved on. He mentions American whisky, says it tends to flow on Saturday nights and that the men on the base might well come out here in the night and assault the women.

The women ignore this. They stay where they are.

It gets cooler, damper, September after all. Someone asks can they light a fire on a square of concrete. They get permission to. Some of the men from the base even help the marchers set up a standpipe at the water main under a manhole across the road.

Everything is still quite friendly right now. Later there'll be arrests. There'll be court appearances. There'll be sentences in Holloway, a place the protesters will find luxurious in terms of food and heat compared to conditions at the camp. There'll be attacks in the press the vitriol of which will be on a fouler level than the country's yet seen in its tabloid media. There'll be abuse that's meant to terrify, screamed by the military at the protesters. There'll be regular routings, regular destruction of everything in the camp by the bailiffs, regular shredding of all the protesters' possessions, regular scuffles with the military and the police. There'll be a rising level of police violence. There'll be regular middle of the night visits from the local thugs who'll poke burning sticks through the tents made of polythene and branches, and pour pigs' blood and maggots and all forms of excrement including human, of course, over the protesters.

There'll be a local council threatening to confiscate their teabags.

But not yet, not now, none of this right at the start, when the powers that be don't imagine this protest is going to make a difference to anything, never mind be such a big part of the shifting political opinion about nuclear weaponry which will culminate in international policy, within a decade, altering considerably.

They sit round the open fire.

They draw up a chain gang rota for Sunday, Monday, Tuesday.

While they're doing this, it gets decided; the decision just happens. They'll make this protest a permanent one. They'll stay here doing this for as long as they physically can. Even till Christmas, one woman says

(though in the end there'll be a peace camp here, in one form or another, for the next two decades).

It began with thirty six women, several children and a straggle of supporters of both sexes, walking 120 miles in ten days.

Once, on the way, some of the marchers garlanded themselves in flowers from the hedgerows they were passing. A man said this to them when they got to the stopping place in the next town: *when you walked in, you looked like goddesses.*

It's by no means the last time they'll be seen as mythical.

Some of the others on this first night take turns being chained to the fence, swapping places as unobtrusively as possible so nobody from the base will make a dash for them to remove them and disrupt the protest. The four women who've been there all day get clean and get a chance to have something to eat.

Then they chain themselves up again and sleep that night where they are, against the fence.

The others sleep in the chilly woods on and under thin sheets of plastic.

In the middle of the night Art wakes up from a dream.

In it he is being chased by giant monstrous flowers.

He runs as fast as he can but he knows they're closing in on him; he'll be lucky if he gets away without being eaten alive. The insides of the head of the one closest behind him, he knows without turning to look, is open, ready to swallow him whole, petals like jaws, stamen erect and quivering and the size of a battering ram.

There's an old church. He runs for its door, closes it behind him, stands in the damp empty echo. He sees a lot of tombs with the shapes of sleeping people on them and one tomb that's just a box without the shape of a person already on it. Great. He lies down on top of it flat on his back and presses his hands together in the prayer way that the others on top of the tombs have their hands. There. He has metamorphosed into a memorial knight in an armour of stone. Those flowers won't want to swallow him now. What flower can swallow stone?

But the giant flowers come crowding into the church trailing earth off their roots all over the pews and up the middle aisle where there are also people buried under the flagstones, disrespectful of them to drop their soil like that, and now he realizes he's really in trouble *because* he's wearing an armour made of stone, trapped inside it, can hardly move at all, can only watch as the giant swaying flowerheads surround his tomb waving their leaves like obscenities in the churchy air, opening and shutting their mouth-petals.

He addresses the flower monsters through a mouth he can himself no longer open, stony and shut, his hands pressed palm to palm as if glued like that, like he once saw a hypnotist on TV make people do to see how susceptible they'd be to the techniques of hypnosis.

He is so fucking susceptible.

Stop bullying me. I *am* political. It's pathetic. Look at you, all mouth and stamen. Look at me, stiff as stone. What would Freud say about this dream?

He is literally saying the last of these sentences out loud when he opens his eyes in the dark.

His erection subsides.

He sits up.

Where is he?

He is in Chei Bres, his mother's huge house in Cornwall. Whatever that means.

He gets up when his eyes accustom and he can see the shape of the room. He finds the switch by feeling along the wall by the door. The room lights up in all its emptiness.

He doesn't want to have to turn on his phone to see what time it is. There's a smell of something cooking. But it's still dark out.

The stranger, Lux, isn't here.

Well, she wouldn't be, would she?

He has no idea where she'll be. This house has so many rooms, he still has no idea how many. The downstairs rooms are full of the usual stuff, the stuff you expect, done out like a normal house. All the upstairs rooms are as empty of stuff as an empty house's rooms.

He has been curled up on the floor in this one in some bedding they found in a cupboard.

Lux found the bedding. She sorted a room for Iris.

Last night she called him a wanker though (and she's in his employment so really ought to be being more polite). Also, although she's a total stranger, she rather too much presumed to think she'd know better than he does how to deal with his mother.

153

I'll handle it, he'd said.

You don't handle a mother, Lux said.

You do if you're from my family, he said.

But when Lux (who, yes, annoyingly, did know better last night how to handle his mother) had persuaded her to take off all those layers of coat and scarf, his mother had been revealed as frighteningly thin. She is much thinner than the last time he saw her. She is as thin as that thin film star on the perfume advertising (which you have to hope for the actress's sake has been digitally enhanced).

He turns over in the duvet on the floor in the empty-smelling room.

Well. His mother's thinness is her choice.

Choice? (Fuck off, Charlotte.)

And if his mother is curious and asks, which she is quite likely to do, about their sleeping arrangements, he will say it is his and Charlotte's practice to sleep separately and that this is actually quite widespread, something more and more couples are just coming round to doing these days.

What is remarkable about seeing old Iris again is how astoundingly like his mother he can now see she is, even though at the same time they really aren't at all like each other. But they are, in the strangest ways, how they sniff, and move about, his aunt the image of his mother but his mother magnified, as if fulfilled. No, filled full.

He opened his mother's front door at 2am to

what looked like a huge box full of fresh things floating by itself in the air. Potatoes, parsnips, carrots, sprouts, onions.

Artie, she said. Take this box so I can get a look at you.

There she was. Rough-elegant Iris.

You look fine, she said.

You'll need to take your shoes off, he said.

And bloody lovely to see you again too, she said.

The legendary black sheep. Here. It is a gorgeous joke, a sacrilege. It serves Sophia right for acting up like that in front of Charlotte.

Even if she's not the real Charlotte.

What's she like, your aunt, then? Lux asked him last night.

He shrugged.

I don't know her that well, he said. I hardly know her at all. But a couple of years back she followed me on Twitter and friended me on Facebook. She's the kind of person who calls people darling when she doesn't know them, not like an upper class person or a theatre person, I mean the working class way. Not that she was ever working class.

Why don't they speak to each other? Lux said.

Mythologizer.

His mother's voice, in the car all the years ago after his grandfather's funeral.

Deranged. Nobody who isn't deranged can live

*like she does. Psychotic. Psychotic people see the
world in terms of their illusions and delusions,
Arthur. You can't expect the world to
accommodate you on your own terms like she
does. You can't expect to live in the world like the
world's your private myth.*

Differences, he said. World views. Incompatible.

He opened the door in the early hours of the
morning to Iris the mythologizer and it's true, she
was like a myth of the bounteous world, off straight
back out to her car to come back with more and
more lovely things, bags and bags of them, butter,
grapes, cheeses, bottles of wine. The last thing she
came in with was a tree in a pot. It wasn't a
Christmas tree, it was just a tree, an ordinary little
tree with no leaves. My star magnolia, she said.
The only tree I've got that would fit in the car. She
balanced its weight against her and held one of the
rounded-end twigs towards Art and Lux. Its ends
were pointed buds some of which looked like they
were covered in hairs or fluff. Next year's flowers,
she said. How are you, Artie? And is this – but this
isn't Charlotte?

She put the tree down. She wiped her hands on
her sides. She shook hands with Lux.

You don't look anything like the Facebook
pictures, she said. That's quite a talent, to be able to
alter what you look like so completely.

Comes naturally to me, Lux said.

A skill I'd give a lot for. Maybe you can teach me, Iris said.

She picked up the tree in its pot and put it into Art's arms, heavy. Find somewhere celebratory for this, she said. (Art, worried about his mother and the earth on the underside of the pot, eventually left it there in the porch.) Now he lies on the floor and marvels at how doing nothing more than holding a tree inside a house, not even the right Christmas kind of tree, just a live tree, in a pot full of earth, but inside a house, had felt weirdly symbolic, maybe even made *him* feel bounteous.

Bounteous: a word of Lux's, one he'd never used in his life, never thought to use or ever had need of, a word that had never even entered his lexicon till yesterday.

He'll make an Art in Nature notebook note of it to remind himself to look up its etymology.

He starts to twitch and itch in the makeshift bed on the floor. The floor being so hard is probably why he woke up in the first place. Now he's lying here wide awake. It is a prime waste of time.

He usually works on something SA4A based if he's awake in the middle of the night.

But he has no computer.

He can't do any work.

He'd use his phone to (though it's easier to miss the detail on).

He daren't turn it on. He is bereft without his

157

phone! But when he did turn it on again last night to text Iris he couldn't help see that the real Charlotte has been tweeting multiple pictures of snapped-off bits of flowering trees in an array of people's gardens and the text underneath went *I cannot tell a lie it was me who chopped down your winter cherry tree send bill or angry comments here.*

That'll be where the flower dream came from.

What would Freud say.

God almighty. It is the dregs, really, to be living in a time when even your dreams have to be post-postmodern consciouser-than-thou.

That might make a good political Art in Nature subject. He will make a note of it.

He sits up in the mess of bedstuff and wonders what message Charlotte will send the world from him today. Christmas message. Like the Pope's, the Queen's. The real Charlotte. The fake Art.

Iris had texted him straight back which was very gratifying in front of even a fake Charlotte. Thirty seconds is all it took Iris. *On way x Ire.*

Bring food if convenient, he'd texted back, because Lux told him to.

And thank her, Lux said.

How annoying. But he did, because it was a good idea to: thank u ire.

Wanker.

Well, he knows it wasn't meant rudely, not really.

He wonders if she's got piercings in the places not so readily visible, beneath her clothes.

What kind of work do you actually do at your work? she'd said to him on the train yesterday. What's your day like?

I sit at the table in front of my screen, he said.

He explained how he'd spend a certain portion of the day net-surfing. He told her about how he used to do this anyway, before someone offered to pay him to do it, and that one day he'd clicked by chance on some films of close-ups of the stuff in the gaps between cobblestones by an artist in Portugal, which used, as soundtrack, music whose copyright belonged to SA4A.

So you were just watching films and then you thought, I wonder who owns the copyright for this music, Lux said.

Yep, Art said. And I looked it up, it was copyright SA4A, so I wrote to alert them and got offered a job. Simple as that.

Why did you do that? Lux said.

Do what? Art said.

Why did you look it up to see who owned the copyright? Lux said.

I just did, Art said. I had a hunch.

He told her the visual artist had made no mention of permissions in his credits. So he'd checked then emailed SA4A.

Why? Lux had asked.

Art shrugged. Because I could, he said.

Because you could, Lux said.

And the films, Art said. Something about them annoyed me.

What annoyed you? Lux had said.

I don't know, Art said. It wasn't so much the films as the fact that, well, there they were. On the net. Holding forth. Like they mattered.

You were envious of the artist's creativity, Lux said.

No, no, he said. Of course not.

He said it rather loftily.

It was nothing to do with envy. In any case, almost nobody had even watched the films. They'd had like forty nine views. It was uh much more that laws, like copyright laws, are in place for good reason.

I get it, Lux said. You're like the security men who wander about in the places in London that look like they're public places but are really privately owned and don't belong to the public at all.

And in any case, he said. It wasn't nature, in his films. He was calling them nature films. But there was no nature in them.

Ah, Lux said.

They were just films of, like, grit, and litter, Art said.

I see, Lux said. What *he* did went against *your* nature.

Art was tiring of talking about it. He explained in as shorthand a way as possible that SA4A had had the Portuguese man's so-called nature films removed from the net, had sued the artist for quite a lot of money and then, to his own surprise, a SA4A bot had amazingly been instructed by the SA4A team to email Art back personally with a job offer and what turned out to be a fairly lucrative contract.

I get bonuses when I find anything useful for them, he said. It's not commission work. I mean, commission work'd be impossible to live on, obviously.

Obviously, she said.

The nature of the job, he said, is very needle-haystack. I mean, the whole wide world on the web is full of rights transgressions. But you have to track them down. It's not like they're there on a plate. You have to keep looking, keep your eyes peeled. In any case it's not my be-all and end-all, the job, it's just what I do to pay the mortgage. The real job I do, the thing that matters to me most, is write about nature –

About the nature of your job? she said.

– no, nature. Nature itself. The wilds, and weather, things like the, yeah, what's happening to the environment, the planet, I'm really quite political in that writing, at least I'm getting more so, I mean I will be when I get back to it. I'm actually taking a well-earned break from it at the moment.

Lux had nodded and asked did the planet in any form, or the weather, the environment, ever read *him* online and threaten to sue him for writing about it or using bits of it in his work?

First he laughed. Then he realized she was actually waiting for an answer to this ludicrous question.

Well, I'm never contravening anyone's or anything's copyright, am I? he said. How could I be? The world isn't copyrighted. Weather isn't copyrighted. Flowers in hedges, fallen leaves, birds, UK butterflies, puddles, the common midge. These are just some of my more recent subjects. They aren't copyrighted.

Puddles, she said.

Snow, he said, I'm going to write about snow. The next time snow falls. Snow isn't copyrighted. I think I'm safe in saying. Yet.

Can I read one of your writings? she said.

They're on the net, he said. You can read as many as you like, any time you like. Anyone can.

Then she'd asked him did he know about the fields where researchers left dead human bodies out to rot especially to see what happens when we decompose in real weather conditions in the open air.

No, he said. He didn't. How interesting.

He'd got out his notebook and made an Art in Nature note about it.

Imagine, she was saying while he made the note, a field like that, but full of all the finished-with machines.

What machines? he said putting his notebook back into the front pocket of his rucksack.

The old ones, she said. All the things people don't use any more. The big computers from ten years ago, no, less, five years ago, from last year even, I mean all the obsolete things, the printers no one can connect to any more, the boxes with the screens built into them, all the things that have outdated.

Art got his notebook out again and began to write some things down. When he finished writing he closed the notebook but kept it out in case she said something else interesting or useful.

I like to picture them in my head, she was saying, I like to think about them scattered in a field and scientists going round studying them.

They never die, those things, he said. They take them all abroad, the things we update by buying the next model. Nothing is wasted. They recondition the outdated ones and give them to, like, third world countries or places where people are poorer, places that don't have the same access to a speedy technological progress as we do. At least, that's what I believe happens.

She shook her head.

The world, she said and smiled. Bounteous. But that's what it's all about, isn't it?

What? he said. The world being bounteous?

No, she said. What we believe is happening.

On a wet Wednesday in April in 2003 Art and his mother are in the front row of the church at the funeral of his grandfather. There is what his mother calls a good turnout, though behind them the church is half empty.

One of the people from the funeral director's stops at their pew with a woman he's brought up to the front. She sits down beside them.

Artie, the woman says to him.

Hi, he says.

Soph, she says to his mother.

His mother nods but doesn't look.

She will be some friend of his mother's from when she lived here, someone who met him when he was a baby.

She sits back when his mother gets up to go to Communion and she gives Art a big sad smile. She is kind of cool, for an older person. She is wearing a parka. It's a dark-coloured parka, so it's not too disrespectful, though underneath she's wearing a bright white trouser suit. After the funeral she stands next to his mother at the church door and lots of people shake her hand as if they know her. Occasionally a person in the queue of people paying their respects will greet her warmly, even hug her. Nobody hugs his mother or him quite like that; she must be someone more local who knew his grandfather, and he himself doesn't know any of these people. He only knew his grandfather a little, from the meals in hotels in London when he was home from school and his grandfather was down in the city. There are some photos of him when he was too small for school and stayed here with his grandfather when his mother was working.

Wet clothes drying in front of a fireplace, he says on the drive north to have the funeral when his mother asks him what he remembers of that time. There was steam coming off them and he drew in it, on the window, he drew a street and houses and a park and cars and people on the street, and a dog, a really good dog, in it.

His mother makes a sad noise that's also a laugh.

I filled that house with expensive central heating and what did he do? Never switched it on. Even when I offered to pay the bills, she says. Electric bar fire in the living room. Calor gas heater in the kitchen.

He's the only one of my grandparents I actually got to meet, and now will ever have had the chance to meet, Art says.

Well, that's life and time for you, his mother says.

Tell me something you remember about him from when you were small, Art says.

No, his mother says.

Art frowns. He sits back.

His mother audibly sighs. Then she says:

I remember once I was walking through town with him. Which was rare enough, because he was always at the office, we almost never did anything with him on a weekday except on our holidays, first fortnight of July. Well, we were for some reason walking along on this one particular day, dressed in our good clothes, I can't remember why, and there was a lorry delivering stock to a pub and a couple of crates of bottles tipped and fell off the back and hit the pavement. And my father, he dived for the ground, he threw his hands over the back of his head like a bomb had gone off.

She indicates left. The sign says ten miles. They are nearly there.

Something to do with what had happened to him in the war, she says.

A couple of miles later she says:

He was very embarrassed about it. Some people stopped and helped him stand up, someone dusted him down.

A couple of miles after that, she says:

I don't think I ever saw him as distressed as he was that day when he thought he'd made a public fool of himself.

Then his mother stops speaking and starts humming a tune and Art knows the doors of the reminiscence have closed, as surely as if the Reminiscence is a cinema or a theatre and the show is over, the rows of seats empty, the audience gone home.

After the church, after watching the putting of the box into the ground in the rain, the ragged flowers laid out over to the side on the cloth that the gravediggers have covered the mound of earth with, green with fake grass on it, he and his mother give an old lady a lift home then they drive back like everybody else to his grandfather's house for the refreshments. His mother has been organizing the refreshments part of today all week. They came across early from the hotel this morning to do the preparing and she left the table covered in the teatowels they'd brought from home with the sandwiches and cakes under them.

When they pull up outside the house the wet street in front of it is shining in the glare off the sun coming through the cloud and they have to shield their eyes. When they can see again they see that the house's front door is already open. Noise and laughter are ringing out into the street.

Christ, his mother says.

What? he says.

Life and fucking soul, his mother says. Excuse my Swahili, Arthur. Come on. Let's get this over with and get home.

When they go inside, the woman who sat beside

him in the church is a blast of whiteness at the centre of the large crowd of people all in black in the front room.

He now suspects she is his mother's sister, a sister he had no idea she even has, because of what the priest said in his talk about his grandfather in the war, his life after the war in the life assurance business, his late wife, the prizes he won for his dahlias, and how he is survived by his loving daughters *Iris and Sophia*. The woman is telling the room about a song she says was *one of our father's favourites*, she starts singing it, the song about an old lady who swallows a lot of live creatures, a fly, *perhaps she'll die*, then a spider, *perhaps she'll die*, then a bird, a cat, dog, but then the woman makes everyone laugh by including a bunch of animals who aren't part of the original song, a llama, a snake, a koala, an iguana, a lemur, and everybody in the room forgets to be (or to act being) sad and they start roaring in anticipation at what the rhyme might be, roaring with laughter at how much or how little she stretches the line, shouting suggestions, cheering at whatever rhyme she comes up with, right up to the point at which the old lady swallows a horse and when she does everybody shouts out in a kind of delight – even the priest – at how that old lady is now well and truly dead.

Then everybody stands and toasts his grandfather and after that several people come across the room to tell his mother how much her father'd have loved this send-off.

His mother smiles and is polite.

The woman who is his mother's sister gets everybody to join in with the old protest song about how there's a season for everything, and although she is the only person who knows the words about the parts about a time to be born and a time to die, and reap, and cast away stones etc, everybody else joins in with the repeating of the words turn, turn, turn.

He looks over at his mother. His mother is not singing.

You don't remember me, do you? his mother's sister, his aunt, Iris, says to Art when they both happen to be in the kitchen at the same time.

No, Art says. But I know that song you were singing, the one about the lady who swallows the fly. Maybe from TV.

She smiles.

I probably sang it to you, she says. When you were little.

I definitely don't remember that at all, he says. It must've been a really long time ago.

A long time in your life, a short time in mine, she says. That's life, and time, for you. What are you doing with your life and time right now?

I've got exams, he says.

Right, she says. But what are you doing with your *life and time* right now?

Well, I'm working for my exams, he says. I'll need good passes if I want to get into university.

Look, she says. Artie. Don't treat me like a boring distant relative. Not when we've actually spent a quarter of your life so far together.

A quarter of my life? he says.

Albeit the quarter of your life you can least consciously remember, she says. Come on. Tell me something real, try again. I'll ask you again. Ready?

Ready, he says.

So, Arthur, she says in a voice pretending to be a boring relative's voice. How's school, you're boarding, aren't you, is school going well, and what will you be studying when you go to university, and which university will you try for, or do you already have an offer, and what will you plan to do when you graduate, and how much will you earn doing it, and what will you call the three children you'll have with the perfectly lovely wife you're going to marry, which'll probably be the next time we meet in person?

He laughs.

She raises her eyebrows at him as if to say, well?

Right now I'm spending an inordinate amount of the time in my life listening to this, he says.

He gets his iPod out of his pocket.

What is it? she says. A transistor radio?

A what? he says.

He unwinds the earphones and plugs them in. He

switches it on. He scrolls through till he finds track two of Hunky Dory. He hands her the earphones.

A couple of hours later he is lying flat on the back seat of the Audi, still in his black suit. His mother is driving them south again and dropping him back at school. It's getting dark. The way the beads of rain light up in the blackness of the window whenever the car passes under motorway lights makes him feel inordinately childlike.

That's a good phrase. Inordinately childlike. He feels proud of thinking it.

He thinks about how he has now seen a dead person. His grandfather in the coffin looked waxy and unreal. He didn't look anything like anyone Art knew or remembered. The smell of lemon air freshener in the room had made a stronger impression than the seeing of his grandfather as a person who's died, an air freshener stronger, in scent terms, than the flowers in the room.

Surreal was the word. Above real.

Art likes words. One day he'll write them and other people will read them.

Sophia, he says.

Uh huh? his mother says.

He wants to ask her if she's okay. It is her father, after all, who has died. But it feels, what would the word be? Unpermitted.

Instead, he says:

Do you really believe it's God, I mean when you

go to the front and eat the thing they give you like you did today?

She breathes a long breath out.

I went to Communion out of respect for your grandfather and for my upbringing, she says.

But do you believe it? he says. And isn't it disrespectful to God, to do it for grandad rather than God?

I'll let you ask these questions again when and if you ever come home having first studied to become and then finally fully qualified as a theologian, she says.

And the other thing I wanted to ask, he says.

Is it theological? she says.

No, he says. But why did you keep Cleves as your surname rather than take Godfrey's after you married him?

I chose to keep your grandfather's name so as to be able to pass it on to you, she says.

And the last thing I want to ask, he says. Is. Did I really spend quite a lot of time with your sister Iris when I was small?

His mother snorts.

No, she says.

I didn't, he says.

His mother makes a pff noise.

Your aunt, she says. Telling all those people it was his favourite song. Your aunt and my father. I'll tell you about your aunt. She didn't come home for years. She wasn't welcome. He was too angry with her. She didn't even turn up to your grandmother's, my mother's, funeral. Your aunt, my sister, Arthur, is a hopeless mythologizer.

She says some more things about her. Then she doesn't say anything for a bit.

She switches on the radio. Radio 4. People are droning on about a siege that happened exactly a year ago in a church in Bethlehem.

One side says there were hostages in there being held at gunpoint.

The other side says there were no hostages, that no one was being held hostage, that there were just people taking refuge in the church along with some other people who were choosing of their own free will to stay in there with the people taking refuge.

It caused a bit of a drama, when she swallowed the llama.

She swallowed the llama to catch the snake. Think what it'd take to swallow a snake.

It was bigger than a banana but she swallowed the iguana.

She thought it might redeem 'er to swallow the lemur.

It was awfully hard-work to swallow the aardvark.

More than she could chew, the gnu.

Koala. Swimming gala.

Iris had put the earphones in her ears.

Oh You Pretty Things.

He'd pressed play.

Her face lit up so that she looked old and like a child both at once.

Inordinately childlike.

I used to play you this, she shouted so loud that a lot of people turned in the hall to look at them.

She started singing the lines about the nightmares coming and the crack in the sky. Art put his finger to his lips. She stopped singing. She leaned forward still with the song playing in her ears and took him by the shoulders.

I was never any good at keeping quiet, she said in a whisper.

Let's see another Christmas.

This one is the one that happened in 1991.

Art has no memory of it.

It is when he is five years old and living near a place where someone called Newlina's father cut her head off because she wouldn't do what he said. After he did that, she'd picked her head up off the ground and tucked it under her arm and left his house. This story makes his grandfather laugh and laugh when he comes to stay. He laughs till tears come out of his eyes and he puts his arms round Ire. He isn't here right now but he comes quite often. When he does he always brings floral gums, which are sweets that taste of flowers and Ire says the other taste is chemicals.

The other thing the lady with no head could do is simply stick pieces of broken branch in the ground and they'd turn into trees with fruits already on them.

This is where he lives when he is not staying at his grandfather's house.

At this house there is a Christmas tree bigger than he is. It is in a pot so it can go back into the ground when it isn't Christmas any more.

He tells Ire he wants a Game Boy for Christmas. She says when her ship comes in, which means no.

But she gets him one anyway, and gives it to him though it is not quite Christmas Day yet, she says she is not one for rules, and he is fighting her on her lap to get to play with it more than she does, they are laughing and she is tickling him, when the lady who is his mother parks a really big car like a Jeep at the front door, comes into the house and picks him up and carries him out, puts him on its back seat and buckles him in. The seat smells clean. The car smells clean. It *is* really clean. There is nothing on the floor where your feet go, no papers or blanket or books. There is nothing in this car except him and the lady in the front who is his mother.

He tells her about his clothes and the Game Boy. She says they will get new ones in the new place he's going to be living now that he is school age.

He tells her he already has a school and a lot of friends at the school.

She says ah but she has a better school for him, the kind where it's an adventure because you get to live there and be with your friends all the time and not have to come home on the nights and days in between.

They do get new clothes and a new other Game Boy. The new house is really big, so big that you can go from bedroom to kitchen to bathroom and there are still other places to go in it.

The lady who is his mother has a television that is bigger than any television he has ever seen. At his mother's house it is Christmas all week and then it is New Year, on the television.

Christmas Day, near noon. He goes to find his mother in her house full of empty rooms. He knocks on shut doors till she shouts from behind one.

I'm not ready yet, she says. I'll come out when I'm ready to, only when I'm ready to and not before, so don't bother me, Arthur.

He goes down to the kitchen.

Iris is making Christmas lunch. She waves him out.

Go and write a blog or something, she says.

He goes out of doors, down to the barn. Lux is there. It looks like she really did sleep in the barn.

She's made herself a bed up against some boxes. She points to her bare feet.

This is a place with heating in the floor, she says.

She has shifted some of the open stock boxes and crates to one side to make a small enclosure for her bed. One of the open boxes is full of lighting stock.

Look, she says holding up in each hand an anglepoise lamp, the kind manufactured to look like old anglepoise lamps from the past.

Oh good, he says. I could do with one of those. And a bed. Tell me if you come across anything resembling a bed in here.

What *is* all this stuff? she says.

I think it's what was left, he says.

Of what? she says. Why isn't your mother selling it somewhere? There's a fortune in here. Why are these made to look so old when they're brand new?

That's what people like buying just now, he says. Things that look like they've got a history, reclaimed looking things. Or used to like buying, before they didn't have the money to.

Is it all lamps? she says. In all these crates?

Probably not, he says. God knows. Drinking glasses that look like they're from French cafes of the 1960s. Nail brushes and washing-up brushes with wooden handles. Things that look like people kept biscuits or flour in them in the last war. Household stuff that looks like it has a history. Like you can buy yourself a pretend history for your

177

house or yourself. The same balls of string as the ones you can get in the Post Office, except in Make Do they cost £7 instead of £1.50. Patchwork quilts. Mock Victorian tin plaques with the names of chocolate manufacturers on them. You know the kind of thing.

Lux looks blank.

All the money, all the things, all the years, he says. From the kilims she brought in before I was born, before the cultural revolution meant she couldn't any more, which was a cataclysm for her business, all the way to the 1990s dreamcatcher stuff. Did you never shop at Minerva's Owl?

Lux continues to look blank.

In the 90s? he says.

I wasn't here in the 90s, Lux says.

Soapstone animals, buddhas carved out of driftwood, incense sticks, incense cones, raffia. Meditation stuff. Minerva's Owl ate our London house, we had a house by the river when I was at school. She sold everything, including the flat she was living in, to open the Make Do chain. And the Make Do chain did well for a bit, and then?

He makes a sound like an explosion.

But she has here, he says. So she's okay. She has the house. Not on the company books. Largely thanks to him.

He nods his head at the cardboard cut-out of Godfrey. *Oh! Don't Be Like That!* Futurist Theatre

Scarborough twice nightly Tel 60644 Opens Sat 19
June Stalls 75p (15/-) 65p (13/-) 55p (11/-) 45p (9/-).

Your father, Lux says.

That's him, Art says.

You were engendered by a meeting between the
two-dimensional and the three-dimensional,
Lux says.

Ha, Art says. Explains a lot about me.

You are a modern miracle, Lux says.

She puts one unplugged lamp at each side of her
bedding on the floor of the barn.

There, she says. Now we're home.

She sits on her bedding. Art sits next to her.

A good man? she says. Your father.

I don't really know, Art says. There's a sort of
hole in my life, where the word father is. He played
a gay person on TV and in panto; if I had my
laptop I could show you him on YouTube, there's
old film of him on there.

We could watch on your mother's computer,
Lux says.

She'd never permit it, Art says. I mean, she'd
never permit me to use the computer.

I don't think she'd mind, Lux says. We could just
go and look.

In any case, Art says. I don't know the password.

I know the password, Lux said.

No you don't, Art said.

I do, Lux said. She said I could use it.

My mother? Art says. Let you? Use her work computer?

Yes, Lux says.

What for? he says.

I wanted to send a message to my mother, she says. I asked. She said I could.

She's never let me use a computer of hers, not once. My whole life, he says.

Perhaps you never asked, Lux says.

He's about to ridicule this. Then he thinks about it. It could be true. It is possible he has just never asked.

Because I knew I'd be turned down, he says.

Lux shrugs.

She says something with ks and zs in it in another language.

Which means, you don't play, you can't win, she says.

In his mother's office, Lux shows him the piece of paper with his mother's password on it. He types it in, brings up YouTube and looks up the documentary about old theatre stalwarts in which Godfrey has a three minute slot. Godfrey, filmed on stage somewhere in grainy bleached old filmstock, stands as if constricted, his arms crossed over himself and his legs crossed too like a ballet dancer. Then he runs across the stage waving his arms in the air. Don't be like that! he shouts. The invisible audience laughs off camera, off mic, off

acoustic, sounds distant and ghostly. On a clip
from a BBC sitcom from the early 70s Godfrey
grimaces, bats his eyes at the camera in disdain
and wears a cravat. The studio audience erupts.
The big joke is, he works in marriage guidance.
*Ever feel trapped in a farce you can never in a
million years get out of?* he says boredly to the
camera as a young tall blonde actress comes in on
the arm of a bald man whose head only comes up
to her sizeable chest. Triplets, Godfrey says. Art has
watched this video many times. The studio
audience laughter is always a bit like being hit with
a blunt instrument; every time the camera does a
close-up on Godfrey pulling his long horse face
even longer, every time he says even just a part of
his catchphrase – oh! don't be! – the laughter is
thick as a mallet.

Lux frowns. The audience laughs again.

What are they laughing at? she says.

Sacrifice, Iris says.

Iris has come into the room behind them and has
been watching Godfrey too over their shoulders.

I think he was a very nice bloke, Godfrey Gable,
she says. I only met him the once but sometimes
once is enough to know. A very intelligent man, I
think now. He knew exactly what he was doing.
There's good money in humiliation. Of course,
you'll know this already, Artie. His real name was
Ray, Raymond Ponds. After they were married the

papers pretty much left him alone. No story. Especially after your mother had you.

Art nods as if he knows (though he really only knows anything about Godfrey from the mentions he got in the books Charlotte had for her dissertation).

And now for our entertainment when we want humiliation we've got reality TV instead, Iris says. And soon instead of reality TV we'll have the President of the United States.

She holds out an iPad to Art.

Thought you should see your latest tweet, she says. According to your feed you've just told 16,000 people that a bird that's usually only resident in Canada's been seen in a rare sighting today off the coast of Cornwall.

How has he told 16,000? He only has 3,451 followers. He takes the iPad. 16,590 followers. As he looks at the screen the number rises to 16,597.

Canadian warbler alert in UK, he reads. *Blown off course map co-ords in next tweet MERRIEST XMAS EVER to all tweeby birders.*

Anyone who knows will know it's Canada warbler. Not Canadian.

Charlotte, he says. I'll kill her.

No violence necessary, Iris says. Just tell her to stop it. Here she is, right here.

Art nearly chokes on his own in-breath.

I'm a different Charlotte, Lux says. His other Charlotte.

She winks at Iris.

Oh, his *other* Charlotte, Iris says. Well, far be it from me to tell anyone what to do. But if I were you, Artie, I'd tell the Twitter people. I mean report it to the organization. Someone who's not you is pretending to be you.

I will, Art says. I intend to.

Unless you're not you, Iris says, and the real you is elsewhere tweeting. Well? Are you you?

I'm me all right, Art says. I'm more me than I care to admit.

Me, me, me, Iris says. It's all your selfish generation can ever talk about. I'm going to tweet about it in a long scroll unrolling itself out of my mouth like in an illustration of a dandy by an eighteenth century satirist. No, I mean like a president. I'll do it presidentially. I mean a fake president, I'll do it fake presidentially.

Art's chest contracts.

She knows, he thinks.

His heart sinks.

Everybody knows the fake I am.

It was a balmy October late afternoon three years ago. I have, as you will already know if you follow this blog of mine, been thinking about writing about puddles for quite some time now and voila today I am about to write about for you now was the first day that I decided that I would begin studying them in practice.

I was driving west out of the city to go and see some puddles in the wilds, for I was tired beyond tiredness of city puddles, which never remind me at all of my boyhood, or of anything about it, which means I loom in them rather than look in them if you see what I mean, which believe it or not was a moment ago I admit just a mistake I made with my keyboard, loom for look, but is now, by the muddle of all true things that happens all the time, meaningful in its own right. [NB this word muddle. It will becomes important in a moment.]

Anyway as chance and luck and fate would have it I was by myself that afternoon having had a sad and painful break-up with 'E', the woman with whom I had been going out with, and I was feeling something more profound than melancholy, something like a boat that has been cut adrift from its worn mooring on a fetid pond in a misty fog, and so I had decided this warm afternoon in October that I wanted to see some untamed puddles, by which I mean puddles not on pavements outside shops in urban settings, but, puddles like the ones that the birds come to drink from and to splash their colourful wings in in old-time poems written by people who lived in the *country not the citified poems, about puddles the citified birds drink at and ablute in.*

Here is what I like to call the history-poem or poem-history of the etymology of the word Puddle. If you are not interested in the history of words then best to skip the next paragraph. You Have Been Warned.

Puddle the word comes from pudd the Old English word for a furrow or a ditch, and puddle its Middle English diminutive with the addition of 'le' making it diminute. Old German has a word Pfudel, which in Old German means a pool of water. Puddle also means a muddle and can also bear the meaning of a muddler according to a dictionary I own that's not online, and that, I take it, is why we associate puddles and mud, a muddle of ground and water perhaps!

I drove speedily out of the city or as speedily as the M25 will legally allow and I took the exit at Junction 15 and I stopped off in a small village off the dual carriageway the name of which I do not recall, for I was about to have a moment which wiped everything else of detail from my mind as I looked at one of the stony path puddles on the way to a generous spread of parkland, where there was still a buzzing of insect life and a proliferation of things growing even though it was now autumnal and this could so clearly be seen in the shadows thrown by the sun's angle to the earth.

I looked into the brown black liquid left by the rainfall on the surface of the path and I felt that at last my childhood had come to mean something more than it had done previously that day or any other day.

For when I was a boy there was a game I liked to play of launching twigs in one of the big puddles which doubled for me as ocean in the summer holidays in the place where cars were parked near my home. I stood at the edge of this puddle in the fading light of the year and of my own years – for I am now so much older than I was when I was a little boy – and I launched some twigs I had gone and broken off a nearby hedge for this purpose. And I watched them as they sailed across the puddle.

And my love for velocity and for life, life itself, returned to me that October afternoon as strongly as it had been and done when I was that boy and am that man.

Art in nature.

Lux clears her throat.

It doesn't seem very *like* you, she says. Not that I know you that well. But from the little I know.

Really? Art says.

They are sitting in front of his mother's computer in the office.

You don't seem so ponderous in real life, Lux says.

Ponderous? Art says.

In real life you seem detached, but not impossible, she says.

What the fuck does that mean? he says.

Well. Not like this piece of writing is, Lux says.

Thanks, Art says. I think.

What I mean is, it doesn't read like the real you, she says.

Oh, it's the real me all right, Art says. No getting away from it, I'm afraid.

What are you afraid of? Lux says.

No, no, it's just a figure of speech, Art says.

What kind of car was it? Lux says.

How do you mean, car? he says.

What I say, Lux says. Car. The one you drove to the puddle in.

I haven't got a car, he says.

So you hired a car? she says. Borrowed one?

I can't drive, he says.

How did you get to the village in the blog then? she says. Someone drove you?

I didn't actually go anywhere. I looked it up on Google Maps and on an RAC route planner, he says.

Ah, she says. But the thing about liking sailing the sticks across the water. That's real. Yes?

It's not a personal memory I myself have, specifically, no, he says. But it's a good general sort of invented shareable memory for the people who'll read the blog.

And was it a balmy October day? she says, or is that made up too?

That's to help people situate themselves inside the piece of writing, he says. It really helps to tell a reader a where or a when and to give a little detail of it.

But none of it is real? Lux says. Not one thing I've just read?

You sound like Charlotte, he says.

It's my job to, she says.

She says I'm not the real thing too, Art says.

I'm not talking about *you* not being real. I'm talking about *this* not being real, Lux says.

The act of it is real to me, he says. It kind of keeps me sane.

Lux nods. She looks at him with what afterwards, when he remembers this talk, he will think of as gentleness.

She looks at the screen again. She doesn't say anything for a moment. Then she says:

I get it. I do. I see. Okay. Now. Tell me something that really did happen, I mean a real thing, not a blog thing, and just a little thing, but something you do remember. I mean from when you were really the boy you imagine you are in that memory you made up about the twigs and the puddle.

A real thing? he says.

Any real thing, she says.

Okay, Art says. Well. I remember being on

somebody's knee, I don't remember whose. I'm holding the edge of the sleeve of what she's wearing, it's wool but it's like lace, like wool with a repeating pattern of holes in it. I'm holding the holes and she's telling me about a boy in a story and the boy is looking up at a sheet of ice so high it's like a cliff face and he's knocking on it with his small hand as if the ice is a door.

Lux shrugs.

There, she says. That's it. Why don't you write exactly that?

Oh I couldn't ever write something like *that* and put it online, he says.

Why not? Lux says.

It's way too real, Art says.

Christmas lunchtime. His mother has refused to come out of her room for him. She has also refused to come out of her room for Lux. ('Charlotte'.) But right on cue she appears in the doorway leaning on the lintel like a fading Hollywood star at the moment Iris starts bringing food through and putting it on the table.

Soph, Iris says.

Iris, his mother says.

Long time, Iris says. How are you?

His mother raises her eyebrows. She puts her hand up to the side of her face. She sits down at the set table.

I shan't be eating much, she says.

Well, that's pretty evident just looking at you, Iris says.

Don't you like food, Mrs Cleves? Lux says.

I suffer, Charlotte, from what some would call the apprehension and I call the knowledge that everything I eat is poisonous to me, his mother says.

What a terrible thing, Lux says. Whether it's apprehension or knowledge or both.

You understand me perfectly, his mother says.

Jealousy and annoyance course through Art. He says nothing. Iris comes through with a tray of roast potatoes and sits down. Everybody clinks a glass to Christmas except his mother who has refused wine.

I took the room the birds used to live in, Iris says.

All a little different now, his mother says as if speaking generally to the room.

I have good memories of this place, Iris says. Did you renovate it, Soph?

Iris used to live here? Really? But his mother is speaking as if she's a tour guide, as if the room is full of strangers and there is a wall of glass between her and them.

I bought the house and grounds as you all see them today, she says, after someone else had brought it handsomely back to life from a state of disrepair and near-demolition. I was impressed with the vision of the people who'd renovated. I'd known the house formerly, some years back, of course. When I came to see it again I was pleasantly met with it in this much better state.

Iris looks round the dining room.

This was the orangerie, she says. Used to be all windows along that wall and they looked straight out south facing into the garden, a dream. I was wondering who thought to take all that light out of here.

She turns to Art.

It's not where we lived, though. That was before your time. You and I lived in Newlyn. We used to visit the pit they dug to commemorate the miners who died, the place with the grassy seats. Remember?

I don't, he says.

Never mind. I do, Iris says.

As soon as Iris goes through to the kitchen his mother leans forward.

You never lived with her, Arthur. He never lived with her, Charlotte. He lived with my father for a bit, when he was pre-school and I was regularly out of the country. But never with her.

His mother puts one Brussels sprout and one half-potato on to her dinner plate. She pours a little gravy to the side of them. Everybody else eats. His mother doesn't touch either the potato or the sprout. She dips her fork in the gravy and puts its tips on her tongue.

Nobody says anything, till Lux/Charlotte, who has been watching his mother not eating, says:

I have something I wonder about Christmas.

What? Art says.

What I wonder about is the manger, Lux says. Why did they put the baby in a manger? I mean in the song and the story?

It's not a song or a story, his mother says. It's the beginnings of Christianity.

Well, I'm not a Christian, and I'm not up on all the ramifications, Lux says. But what I'm asking is. Why is it a manger?

Poverty, Iris says.

No crib for a bed, his mother says. There were no beds available anywhere.

Yes, but why the emphasis on it being a *manger* in particular? And why is the little Lord Jesus, in the song at least, I mean, *away* in one? Lux says.

It's just the idiom of the time the carol was written, Art says. Wait. I'll check on Google.

He gets his phone out. But then he remembers he doesn't want to switch his phone on.

He puts it face down next to his plate and frowns.

Google, his mother says. The *new* new found land. Not so long ago it was only the mentally deranged, the unworldly pedants, the imperialists and the naivest of schoolchildren who believed that encyclopaediae gave you any equivalence for the actual world, or any real understanding of it. And door-to-door salesmen sold them, and they were never to be trusted. And even the authorized encyclopaediae, even them we never mistook for or accepted as any real knowledge of the world. But now the world trusts search engines without a thought. The canniest door-to-door salesmen ever invented. Never mind foot in the door. Already right at the heart of the house.

On the other hand, Iris says, here's something I stumbled on, on the net, just last week.

She gets out her own phone and presses and swipes its screen.

If you get a choking feeling and a smell of musty hay, you can bet your bottom dollar that there's phosgene on the way. But the smell of bleaching powder will inevitably mean that the enemy you're meeting is a gas we call chlorine. When your eyes begin a twitching and for tears you cannot see, it's not mother peeling onions, but a dose of C.A.P. If the smell resembles pear drops then you'd better not delay. It's not father sucking toffee, it's that ruddy K.S.K. If you catch a pungent odour as you're going home to tea, you can safely bet your shirt on it they're using B.B.C. D.M., D.A. and D.C. emanate the scent of roses, but despite their pretty perfume they aren't good for human noses. For it's mustard gas, the hellish stuff that leaves you one big blister, and in hospital you'll need the kind attention of the sister. And lastly, while

*geraniums look pleasant in a bed, beware this smell
in wartime. If it's lewisite you're dead.*

Halfway through the recitation his mother puts
her fork, which she's been holding in the air, down
hard next to her plate hitting its edge.

From the 1940s, Iris tells them. Not something
you're likely ever to have found in any of those old
encyclopaedias. It was given to schoolchildren to
learn off by heart to help them recognize what they
might be breathing into their lungs in a gas attack.
Welsh schoolkids were given the same poem in
Welsh.

My sister the internet hipster, his mother says.
The internet. A cesspit of naivety and vitriol.

Well, the naivety and the vitriol were always
there all along, Iris says. The internet's just made
them both more visible. That's maybe a good thing.
God. If we're talking vitriol. You should see some
of the letters I've had over the years.

Art's mother yawns an ostentatious yawn.

Art borrows Iris's phone so he can look up
something and change the subject. What he looks
up is Away in a Manger. He reads some Wikipedia
facts about it out loud. Then he looks up the words
significance, *jesus* and *manger*. The phone suggests
a site called compellingtruth.com. The site
won't load.

Because, Lux is saying. Could it be that
consumerism and Christmas lunch are both related

not just to each other but directly to that tiny baby too for whom there's apparently no room anywhere in a town and because of this ends up being put in a manger?

And we won't go until we've got some, his mother sing-says.

It Came upon the Midnight Clear's my favourite, Iris says. Two thousand years of wrong. And man at war with man hears not. Then the angels sing, the angels bend to earth. I like a flexible angel.

I think you'll find it's The Holly and the Ivy, his mother says, that's the only truly truthful Christmas carol.

Because it's really important, the most important thing about a Christmas carol, that it be truthful, Iris says.

Art sees his mother's face flinch.

And anyway, I was also wondering, how is it okay, Lux is saying, okay in any way, to be wishing everybody peace, peace on earth, goodwill to all men, merry, happy, but just for today, or only for these few days a year? And if we can do it for a few days, why can't or won't we do it all the year? I mean. That story of the football match between enemies in the First World War in the trenches. It reveals it. The stupidity.

It's gestural, Art says. It gestures to hope.

But it's empty gestural, Lux says. Why would you not work all the time for peace on earth and goodwill? What's the point of Christmas, otherwise?

The Christmas shopping weeks, beginning in July, are the point, Art says.

Lux rolls her eyes. Iris grins at her and then at Art.

I suppose what I'm saying, Lux says, I mean about the manger, is. Is it a manger they put the baby in because the baby's going to be eaten in the end? Is being eaten the destiny of that baby from the very start?

Oh, you're bright, Iris says. She's a bright one, Artie. See the tender lamb appears. Promised from eternal years.

Not that we've seen any meat at all this lunchtime, his mother says.

That's because it's everything I happened to have in the house and brought with me that we're eating, Iris says, and you're an old miserly grump who had nothing in the house for your son and his girlfriend for Christmas except a bag of walnuts and half a jar of glacé cherries.

She says it amiably, like a joke. But the air round them in the room thickens like cooling gravy.

Though perhaps *you'd* like to eat those cherries and nuts, since you seem to be eating nothing else on the table in front of you, Iris says. I can nip through and get them for you, shall I?

Lux leans across the table to speak to his mother.

I happen to be a vegetarian, she says, and it's been a very nice meal indeed and a great relief to come here and be able to join in with your family meal at Christmas time and meet such hospitality down to the last detail, Mrs Cleves. Try some of these parsnips, on your side plate.

They have seen butter, his mother says.

They really have, Lux says. They're what people call heavenly.

Then no, thank you, Charlotte, his mother says.

Soph prefers hell, Iris says.

But I will have a piece of bread, his mother says. Thank you, Charlotte.

Iris holds out a basket of bread. When his mother doesn't take a piece, Iris laughs and passes the basket to Art, who holds it in front of his mother, who still doesn't take a piece. Art passes it to Lux, who holds it out. His mother immediately takes a piece.

And it strikes me, forgive me, Lux says while taking care, Art notices, to put the basket down near his mother who takes another piece almost immediately, surreptitiously, and eats it very fast like a squirrel. That this room right now is reminding me a bit of the play by Shakespeare where all through the story someone will step forward and say something which the person reading the play, or I suppose the audience, is meant to hear and know about but the other people on the

197

stage when it's being said for some reason *can't* hear, or are meant to *act* like they can't hear, even though the person who's speaking says it really plainly and everybody in the theatre hears it.

I think you mean panto, not Shakespeare, Art says. Where people in the audience all join in and boo the villain when he comes out on to the stage.

No I don't, Lux says. The one where there's the king and the lying step-queen, and the king's daughter, and a man who hides in a box in the daughter's room then gets out of the box in the middle of the night so he can take a look at her with nothing on, and steal some stuff to prove he's been there, and then he tells lies about sleeping with the daughter to the daughter's husband who's been banished abroad, all to win a bet and make some money, and the queen, who's her stepmother, is trying to kill her because she hates her, and now the daughter's exiled husband is trying to kill her too because he's furious, so the daughter disguises herself as a boy and goes into the woods, where a woodsman is supposed to murder her on the order of her husband, who has believed the lies he's been told about her sleeping with someone else.

Oh God. To make herself seem more like the imagined Charlotte, presumably, Lux is making up a terrible bland fairytale plot that's nothing like Shakespeare and pretending it's Shakespeare.

But the woodsman is a good man and can't kill

198

her, Lux is saying, and he gives her instead what he thinks is a medicine to keep her safe in the woods alone, but what it actually is, instead, is a poison the queen gave *him*, telling him it was powerful medicine but hoping secretly he'll do exactly this, give it to her stepdaughter. And he does, and he leaves her in the woods, where she meets some wild boys who she doesn't discover till the end of the play aren't wild boys at all but are princes, and not just that, but they happen to be her long lost brothers, and they all live together in the woods for a bit until she feels unwell one day and takes the medicine and she falls into a deep sleep, like death. But it's not death. Because it isn't a poison after all. Because a doctor has been instructed to make it and decided *not* to make a poison even though the queen ordered him to, because he is a man who wants to do no wrong and he thinks the queen is really untrustworthy. Basically she wants to poison everybody. So eventually the daughter who's meant to be dead wakes up.

Phew! Iris says.

And that's only half the story, Lux says. In the rest of it people have visions, a family that's dead comes back and visits, and a god appears on an eagle's back and drops a book down to a prisoner in a jail that tells him what will happen in the future, but all in the form of a riddle he has to solve.

It must be, uh, one of the Shakespeares, Art says, that are very little seen, maybe, or one of the ones that are still in the process of being attributed to him.

Fear no more the heat o'th' sun, his mother says. Golden lads and girls all must, as chimney-sweepers, come to dust. Chimney-sweeper, an old name for the head of the dandelion, a dandelion when it's gone to seed. So beautiful. Cymbeline.

Cymbeline, Lux says.

A play about a kingdom subsumed in chaos, lies, powermongering, division and a great deal of poisoning and self-poisoning, his mother says.

Where everybody is pretending to be someone or something else, Lux says. And you can't see for the life of you how any of it will resolve in the end, because it's such a tangled-up messed-up farce of a mess. It's the first of his plays I read. It also happens to be why I ever wanted to come to this country to study. I read it and I thought, if this writer from this place can make this mad and bitter mess into this graceful thing it is at the end, where the balance comes back and all the lies are revealed and all the losses are compensated, and that's the place on earth he comes from, that's the place that made him, then that's the place I'm going, I'll go there, I'll live there.

Ah, Art says. Yes. Of course. Cimmeleen.

And I was telling you about it, Lux says, because

it's like the people in the play are living in the same world but separately from each other, like their worlds have somehow become disjointed or broken off each other's worlds. But if they could just step out of themselves, or just hear and see what's happening right next to their ears and eyes, they'd see it's the same play they're all in, the same world, that they're all part of the same story. So.

So, Art says. What'll we talk about now? I had this dream last night, it was amazingly vivid.

Iris laughs.

What's it like, living with my nephew? she says.

I've no idea, Lux says.

Ha ha! Art says.

I live most of the time in the warehouse I work in, Lux says.

She's joking, Art says.

They don't know I sleep there, Lux says. I sleep up in one of the empty rooms on the top floor above the office space.

She likes to make stuff up, Art says. She can be very convincing.

The truth is, Lux says, it's a far better job than when I worked for Cleangreen, when I still had to grub about for somewhere to stay from day to day, because Cleangreen didn't have premises, so I spent most of the time on my friend's sofa, but then my friend Alva got a better job and moved to Birmingham and in any case Cleangreen started employing the African people the boss brings over because he doesn't have to pay them anything. And it's miles better working in deliveries and packing than in selling soap, because there's no way you can sleep in the Mall unless you sleep with the security guys. I mean, have sex with. Which I won't. So it's good, the warehouse. But I can't hang out there on my day off, or sleep there on the night I have my day off, unless I can slip past without the night shift noticing.

Art realizes his mouth is open. He closes it.

Why don't you just stay at Art's? Iris says.

She does, Art says. Obviously. Don't you, Charlotte?

Truthfully? Lux says. No.

They live together, his mother says. At least he told me they did. But who am I to know anything about my son? I'm just his mother. Who am I to know anything about his life? Who am I to think I know the truth?

The truth is, we haven't come that far in our relationship yet, Lux says.

I understood it was nearly three years, his mother says.

Oh no, I'm not *that* Charlotte, Lux says.

Oh that's right. You're the other Charlotte, Iris says.

What other Charlotte? his mother says.

Art clears his throat. His mother looks at him.

Why does everybody in this room but me know about there being another Charlotte? his mother says.

It's my fault, Lux says. I specifically asked your Arthur not to mention it to you, Mrs Cleves. Because, uh, because I was shy to come to Christmas here as a family guest so early in our knowing each other. Plus, I don't really think of myself as Charlotte. In fact, I'd prefer it if you'd all call me the name everyone in my own family calls me.

Not Charlotte? Iris says.

Lux, Lux says.

Art rubs the heels of his hands into his eyes. He takes his hands out of his eyes in time to see his mother's face go unexpectedly soft.

Like the soap flakes? his mother says. Oh. Oh how lovely they were. They used to melt in the water and make the water smooth and slippery, remember?

And in the advert on TV they sifted down like snow, Iris is saying. And Soph drew a House of the Future for a school project, didn't you, one where you had to design a Room of the Future, she won a prize for her Future House from the town council, she designed a winter room and a summer room and I helped.

She stuck Lux Flakes on to Sellotape for a textured sheepskin rug for the winter room, his mother says. It was so clever. I can't remember what we did for the summer room.

I can, Iris says. I cut the little pictures out for you off the sleeve of one of the Linguaphone Speak Italian records and stuck them as if they were pictures on its wall, drew frames round them with black ink –

Yes, his mother says. There was a waiter with glasses and a bottle of wine, and a French policeman, and a man climbing the Alps and drinking a beer, and a woman dressed in something traditional, maybe Dutch –

– and we put these on the walls of the Future Summer Room, Iris says, and I had to take the cut-up record sleeve all the way to town to throw it in a litter bin that far from home, I was so scared our father'd find out, and we tucked the extra 45 into one of the other sleeves with a different lesson –

Lezione, his mother says. I suoni Italiani, Professore Pagnini –

Professor Paganini, Iris sings.

They both sing:

Professor Paganini, now don't you be a meanie, what's up your record sleeve, come on and spring it –

They both laugh at the same time.

I drew the sun through the summer room window, Iris says.

We thought the future would be as sunny and cosmopolitan and continental as Italy, his mother says.

She was named for Italy, Iris says.

And she was named for Greece, his mother says.

We were named for the places our father fought in, in the war, Iris says. For Europe.

Oh here we go, here we go, his mother says. I've been waiting to see what the catalyst would be. Any minute now, Charlotte, it'll be all *we grew up on a street named after a battle against fascism*.

Will it? Iris says. Oh, this is good. This'll be entertaining. What else will I say, Soph? Though it's true. We did grow up on a street named after a battle against fascism.

It is strange, Lux says, to think of anyone in this country ever talking about a room of the future when people like so much to buy new things that look like old things, and the only room I'm used to hearing people talk about is the *no* room, the *no more* room.

It's sad but true, Charlotte, his mother says. There *is* no more room.

Says the businesswoman who lives alone in a house that has fifteen bedrooms, Iris says.

His mother goes a furious red.

She speaks only to Lux, as if Iris isn't in the room.

They're economic migrants, his mother says. They want better lives.

The ghost of old Enoch, Iris says in a ghost voice. Rivers of bloo-oOOo-ood.

What's wrong with people wanting better lives, Mrs Cleves? Lux says.

You mustn't be naive, Charlotte. They're coming here because they want *our* lives, his mother says.

I bet I know what you voted, Iris says. In the so-called vote. My sister. The so-called intelligent one. I was the wild one. So-called.

But what will the world do, though, Mrs Cleves, Lux says, if we can't solve the problem of the millions and millions of people with no home to go to or whose homes aren't good enough, except by saying go away and building fences and walls? It isn't a good enough answer, that one group of people can be in charge of the destinies of another group of people and choose whether to exclude them or include them. Human beings have to be more ingenious than this, and more generous. We've got to come up with a better answer.

But his mother is gripping the arms of her chair with fury.

The so-called vote, his mother says, was a vote to free our country from inheriting the troubles of other countries, as well as from having to have laws that weren't made here for people like us by people like us.

Depends whether you think there's a them and an us, Iris says, or just an us. Given that DNA's let us know we're all pretty much family.

Oh there is most definitely a them, his mother says. In everything. Family is no exception.

Philo, Philo, Soph, Soph, Soph, you're such a good girl, Iris says. Thinking exactly what the government and the tabloids tell you to think.

Don't patronize me, his mother says.

It's not me who's doing the patronizing, Iris says. And they're only running away from home for fun. Because that's why people leave home, isn't it? For fun.

There is a moment of silence after Iris says this.

Then his mother says:

I warned you, Charlotte.

Call me Lux, Lux says.

My sister, his mother says, is something of a seasoned protester against the powers that be. She'll be trying to get you all singing next, some song about Mandela, or Nicaragua, or Carry Greenham Home.

Who's Carrie Greenham-Home? Art asks.

Iris laughs out loud.

Does she live locally? Art says.

Iris nearly falls off her chair laughing.

There hanging out in the mud with the lesbians for years, his mother says.

One of the best and filthiest times of my life, Iris says.

I'm a lesbian myself, Lux says.

At heart, she means, Art says.

Yes, at heart too, Lux says.

She's a very empathetic person, Art says.

Does she live locally, Iris says. Nearer home than far away. And talking of locally, I went for a walk this morning down to the village. I passed so many people, closed faces, on the streets. Did one single one of them say Merry Christmas to me?

Probably all recognized you from the 1970s and thought oh God no *she's* back, his mother says.

Iris, blithe, laughs again.

But I can't help but worry for old England, she says. The furious grumpy faces, like caricatures on some terrible sitcom on TV. England's green unpleasant land.

And you worried for England back then, too, his mother says. Nuclear war. And did it happen? No it didn't.

That's because what happened at Greenham changed the world, Iris says.

My sister has always been one to talk herself up and our country down, his mother says. She has always had the tendency to want to put the blame elsewhere for the inadequacies of her own life. But Greenham. Changing the world. Unbelievable hubris. Glasnost, maybe. Chernobyl. But Greenham? I ask you. I give up.

We did, we gave up everything, Iris says. Homes. Lovers. Families. Kids. Jobs. Nothing left to lose. So, of course, we won.

My sister was quite psychotic about banning the bomb, Charlotte, at the time, his mother says.

We're all psychotic about something, Iris says. We all have our visions.

And divisions, Lux says.

We were *all going to die*, his mother says. But in the end? It seems, after all, we didn't. Nuclear holocaust.

She makes a scoffy sound.

We're not out of that quicksand yet, Iris says. Let's see how low the newest leader of the free world can sink us this time round.

His mother stands up. She heaves her chair round to face the other way. She sits down again in it with it facing the wall, with her back to everyone at the table.

Is that you taking back control, there, Soph? Iris says.

The most, eh, amazing dream, Art says. Believe it or not, I was –

Take back control of your teeth, Lux says. I saw it on TV on a commercial. And another: take back control of your heating bills. And there was another: take back control of your rail fares. And bus routes, take back control of your bus routes. That one was painted on the back of a bus.

The funny thing is, Iris says to his mother's back. When I told our father about me cutting those pictures off the little record sleeve for your room of the future, he wasn't angry at all. He laughed and laughed.

His mother's back is now giving off enough anger to fill the whole house.

He'd have hated the vote, our father, Iris says. He was maybe sometimes a foolish old racist himself but he knew a fool's errand when he saw one. He'd have thought it cheap beyond all precedent.

You know nothing about him, his mother says. You have no right to speak about either of them.

Funny you should mention Freud, Art says (though nobody has mentioned Freud). The dream I had last night, this morning, I woke up from it actually saying out loud the word Freud.

He launches in. He refuses interruption. He tells them the whole dream.

After he finishes there's a silence like there is when you've been telling someone a dream and the person you're telling stopped listening several minutes ago and is thinking of something else. His aunt is looking at the wall where there used to be a window. His mother is a turned back. But Lux, who's been rolling pieces of bread into little balls and lining the little balls up in formation like cannonballs outside a castle by her side plate, says:

For you, in that dream, the powers that be turned into the flowers that be.

Ha! Art says.

He looks at Lux.

What a beauty of a thing to say, he says.

Beauty, his mother says to the wall. That's right. Well said, Charlotte. Beauty is the true way to change things for the better. To make things better. There should be a lot more beauty in all our lives. Beauty is truth, truth beauty. There is no such thing as fake beauty. Which is why beauty is so powerful. *Beauty* assuages.

Iris roars with laughter again.

That's it, she says. Never mind recession or austerity. Beauty'll make it better. Good old Philo. I used to call your mother that, Artie, I used to call her Philo when we were kids.

We should all, right now, tell each other one single beautiful thing, his mother says. We should, each person round this table, tell everyone here about the most beautiful thing we've ever seen.

Philo Sophia, Iris says. And I think all these years she's been imagining that what I meant was that she was like a philosopher. But I didn't. I didn't mean philosophy.

She creases her shoulders and laughs.

I meant the pastry kind, she says. The *thin* kind. The kind of pastry you can almost see through, it's so nearly not even there.

My elder sister always did like to disenchant, his mother says.

She says it with considerable dignity even with her back to them all.

211

Okay, I'll start, Lux says, right, the most beautiful thing I have ever seen. It's to do with Shakespeare again. It was *in* a Shakespeare. By which I mean not in the writing but *on* the writing, it was a real thing, a thing from the real world, that someone had at some point in time put inside a copy of Shakespeare.

I was in Canada, I visited a library, we got taken by the school I was at, and they have a very old copy of Shakespeare there, and inside it on two of its pages there's the imprint of what was once a flower that someone pressed between the pages.

It's the bud of a rose.

Well. It's the mark left on the page by what was *once* the bud of a rose, the shape of the rosebud on its long neck.

And it's nothing but a mark, a mark made on words by a flower. Who knows by whom. Who knows when. It looks like nothing. It looks like maybe someone made a stain with water, like an oily smudge. Until you look properly at it. Then there's the line of the neck and the rosebud shape at the end of it.

That's *my* most beautiful thing. Now. You.

She nudges Art.

Your most beautiful thing, she says.

Uh huh, most beautiful thing, Art says.

But he can't think of one, he can't concentrate because of the insistent noise of his mother and aunt.

212

I cannot be near her fucking chaos a minute longer. (His mother talking to the wall.)

Lucky I'm an optimist regardless. (His aunt speaking to the ceiling.)

It is no wonder my father hated her. (His mother.)

Our father didn't hate me, he hated what had happened to him. (His aunt.)

And mother hated her, they both did, for what she did to the family. (His mother.)

Our mother hated a regime that put money into weapons of any sort after the war she'd lived through, in fact she hated it so much that she withheld in her tax payments the percentage that'd go to any manufacture of weapons. (His aunt.)

My mother never did any such thing. (His mother.)

I know she did. I'm the one who helped her work out the percentage every year. (His aunt.)

Liar. (His mother.)

Self-deceiver. (His aunt.)

The idea that only her life counts, only her life makes a difference in the world. (His mother.)

The idea that there might be a world that's not as she perceives it. (His aunt.)

Deluded. (His mother.)

Deluded all right. (His aunt.)

Mad. (His mother.)

Speak for yourself. (His aunt.)

Mythologizer. (His mother.)

I'm not the person here making stuff up about the world. (His aunt.)

Selfish. (His mother.)

Sophist. (His aunt.)

Solipsist. (His mother.)

Swotty little show-off. (His aunt.)

I know what you did with your life. (His mother.)

I know what you did with my life too. (His aunt.)

After which: unexpected silence, the silence that happens when something too real's been said out loud.

Art tries to work out what, but he can't get to it. In any case he doesn't want to get to it. He stops trying. Who gives a fuck what two old women are fighting over?

As of this moment Art has had enough of Christmas. He now knows he never wants to see another Christmas Day again.

What he longs for instead, as he sits at the food-strewn table, is winter, winter itself. He wants the essentiality of winter, not this half-season grey selfsameness. He wants real winter where woods are sheathed in snow, trees emphatic with its white, their bareness shining and enhanced because of it, the ground underfoot snow-covered as if with frozen feathers or shredded cloud but streaked with gold through the trees from low winter sun, and at the end of the barely discernible track, along the dip

214

in the snow that indicates a muffled path between the trees, the view and the woods opening to a light that's itself untrodden, never been blemished, wide like an expanse of snow-sea, above it more snow promised, waiting its time in the blank of the sky.

For snow to fill this room and cover everything and everyone in it.

To be a frozen blade that breaks, not a blade of grass that bends.

To freeze, to shatter, to unmelt himself.

This is what he wants.

But just as he starts to think the word *unmelt* might be a good word for Art in Nature, this happens.

The room darkens. The room fills, or Art's nose does, with a smell of plantlife, the smell of greenness you get when you snap the stem of something living.

Art sniffs. He breathes out. He breathes in again.

It is even more pungent, getting stronger by the second.

Something scatters down on to the table, a shower of little sprinkles of grit, tiny rubble.

Is the ceiling coming down?

He looks up.

A foot and a half above all their heads, floating, precarious, suspended by nothing, a piece of rock or a slab of landscape roughly the size of a small car or a grand piano is hanging there in the air.

Art ducks down.

Jesus Christ almighty.

He looks at the others.

No one else has noticed it.

He dares to look up at it again.

The underside of it is the colour that happens
when black meets green. The size of it throws into
shadow everyone at the table, him too – when he
looks at his own hands in front of him their backs
and the backs of his wrists are black-green.

His mother and his aunt are both shaded. The
girl sitting next to him is cast in dark verdant
shadow too, and she's playing with a piece of bread,
rolling it with her fingers like nothing is happening.

We're all – we're so green, Art says. We're green
as greenfinches.

The slice of landscape hangs above all their
heads. Little bits of rock-dust from the edges of it
crumble down, hit the table and skitter across it like
a giant salt-cellar is seasoning the room and
everything in it. He scratches at his head. There's
grit under his nails when he takes his hand away
from his head. There's grit at the roots of his hair.

He wets the tip of his middle finger in his
wineglass and presses it against the table to pick up
some of the sandy grit. He brings it close to his
eyes. That's exactly what it is, sand. Grit. The slab
of rock is close enough to his head that if he
reached up he could touch it. He can see some mica,

216

something glinting in it where its flint surface is rough. Right there in a crevice directly above Art's head there's a tuft of grassy stuff that's taken root.

It will crush them all when it falls.

But it hangs there. It doesn't fall. It swings slightly in the air. It has heft. Green silence rears beneath it.

Is it real?

Should he say?

But how *can* it just hang like that, suspended by nothing?

Look, he says. Everyone. *Look*.

April:

it is a Wednesday lunchtime, balmy for winter, chilly for spring.

On the concourse in King's Cross Station in London there are two huge Sky News JCDecaux Transvision screens at either end of the departures boards and the screens are promising today's upcoming news headlines after the advertising.

The first headline today in the 20 second news round-up after the 20 seconds of advertising says that there is now *80% more plastic in the earth's seas and on its shores than estimated*, and that this is three times as much plastic as was formerly thought.

The next headline says that there's an *attack taking place on MPs* by MPs of the same party who don't agree with them.

The next headline says that a poll has found that citizens of this country *oppose a unilateral guarantee* for the citizens who live here and who are originally from a lot of other countries to be able to stay here with full rights of residents after a certain date.

Panic. Attack. Exclude.

That's the news part over.

Next on the screen there's an advert for a soft drink, an image of happy looking people drinking it, then an image of a bottle in sunlight, beaded with condensation.

Up on the balcony a man is standing with a hawk on his arm, a working bird he sends back and fore across the station to stop pigeons from thinking they can come in here for scavenging or roosting.

But a buddleia is growing in the wall up next to the roof above the old platforms. It is bright purple against the brickwork.

Buddleia is tenacious.

After the Second World War, when so many of the cities were in ruins, buddleia was one of the most common plants to take hold in the wreckage. The ruins filled with it here and all over Europe.

Art in nature.

3

What's to-day?

   This is happening some time in the future. Art is on a sofa holding a small child in his arms. The child, who has been learning to read, is sitting on Art's knee flicking through a book pulled out at random from the bookcase next to Art's head. It's an old copy of A Christmas Carol by Charles Dickens.

   What's to-day? the child says again.

   It's Thursday today, Art says.

   No, the child says. What's to-day?

   How do you mean, what's today? Art says.

   I mean *this*.

   The child points at the words on the page.

   That's right, Art says. That's what it says. What's to-day.

   I know that's what it says, the child says. But what I want to know. Is. What's to-day?

Today's today, Art says. This is today.

No, the child says. Is the to-day that's written here the same thing as today?

Well, this story is from the past, Art says, so the today it's about is in the past now. And obviously, it's about Christmas, this is a story set at Christmas time, and it's June right now, so this also means it's not the same as today. That's one of the things stories and books can do, they can make more than one time possible at once.

You really aren't understanding me, the child says.

No? Art says.

What I want to know is why does it have the little line between its parts? the child says.

What little line?

Art looks at the page more carefully, at the word the child is pointing at.

To-day.

Ah.

That's just the old way of writing it, Art says. It doesn't mean anything different. It's just that today, I mean nowadays, we don't write the word *today* like they used to. That's the way they used to write it when this book was first published. The little line is called a hyphen.

But I also want to know. What *does it mean* today? the child says.

What do you mean, what does it mean today? Art says.

What I say, the child says.

You *know* what it means, Art says. It means today. And today is, well, it's today. It's not yesterday any more. And it's not tomorrow yet. So it must be today.

But why, when it *sounds* the same, is it *not* the same as to run or to do or to eat? the child says.

Oh, I see, Art says.

And if it *was* the same, how would you day? I want to day. I mean I want to be able to day.

I get you, Art says.

He'll be about to explain the difference between verbs and words like the word today. He'll be weighing up whether the child is old enough to comprehend that we're all simultaneously existing in differently numbered years that depend on things like the country you're in and your religion, though most people across the world agree to go by the Gregorian calendar. He wishes he could remember more about the Gregorian calendar so as to be able to explain it. He'll be about to talk about the human practice of giving names to days to stop the passing of time feeling quite so random. Though this may have to wait for a more mature understanding.

Then again, why underestimate, ever, the mind of a child?

He'll be beginning to think, too, sitting here with the child using him as a climbing frame, about how even if you're drunk, or ill, or mad or drugged or forgetful, or so busy you don't know what day it is, or out of your head on grief or happiness, it's still information easily found, when you need to know what *today* is, there for you on the bar at the top of a computer, on your phone or your watch, if you still use the kind of a watch that tells you days and dates. Or you can always look at the tops of the newspapers on a news stand or in a newsagent's or supermarket.

But now he'll begin to wonder this instead.

How *do* you day?

Regardless of Art thinking anything the child'll be off across the room and out into the garden to look at something moving in the branches of one of the trees, a squirrel maybe, or a bird.

Well, that's a pretty good way to day.

Art sits and watches.

He thinks about how, whatever being alive is, with all its pasts and presents and futures, it is most itself in the moments when you surface from a depth of numbness or forgetfulness that you didn't even know you were at, and break the surface and when you do it's akin to – to what?

To a salmon leaping God knows where, home against the flow, not knowing what home is, not knowing anything except that there's no other thing to do, or to a bird or a bear breaking the surface of winter water with a fish so big in its beak or its mouth that it can't believe its luck, the moment before that fish waggles itself loose, falls away, hits the surface of the water again and disappears back down into it.

Art laughs to himself, his chin down into his chest. He sees and he hears, in the garden, the child yelling in delight at nothing, a bird in a tree.

What's to-day.

It was well after midnight, early Boxing Day
morning, on the top floor in Sophia's house.

Iris opened the door.

What? she said.

Can you please stop making so much noise?
Sophia said. I'm trying to sleep.

I was fucking well asleep, Iris said. The only
noise is you banging on this door.

She went to shut the door on Sophia.

Then who's making the terrible noise?
Sophia said.

What noise? Iris said. There is no noise.

Like someone hammering stone. Moving
furniture about, Sophia said. Like I'm staying in a
hotel and the people on the top floor are
hammering things into concrete and shifting chairs
and tables from one side of the room to the other.

It's the planets in the stratosphere rolling about on purpose just to keep you personally awake, Iris said. How's Artie doing now?

(Arthur had passed out earlier at the dinner table. He had started shouting about landscaping. Then his head hit the table with a thud. They'd brought him round and spent the evening sobering him up.)

Arthur and Charlotte are asleep, Sophia said.

He should know by now not to drink so much, Iris said.

He is ultra-sensitive, Sophia said. It's because he is a late baby. Babies who are birthed by more mature mothers can have greater sensitivities to all sorts of things later in life, including alcohol.

I bet you read that bullshit in the Daily Mail, Iris said.

Sophia blushed (because the Daily Mail was in fact where she'd read it). She changed the subject.

Is this really the room the birds were living in back then? she said.

Iris opened the door wider.

Do come in, she said. Witness my first time sleeping on a floor in quite a while. Me who slept on the floor for decades. But now that I'm classed as old the people I work with, even the people I've gone there to be a help to, are always going out of their way to find me a bed. When nobody else has one. Or to make me one if there isn't one, out of whatever they've got. In places where there are no beds, where people have nothing, they still manage to rustle me up some kind of a bed. So. I must be old.

Are you getting at me for not having a bed in here? Sophia said.

That's right, Iris said, and that's why I'm here. The only reason. To get at you. I left everything behind, all my work, any chance of a Christmas rest, and drove all the way last night and did everything I did today including all the dishes after the lunch I made. All to get at you.

What *are* you working on at the moment? Sophia said.

As if I'd tell you, Iris said.

She sat down on the bedding and patted the blanket next to her. Sophia sat down. There was nothing in the room for Iris to be making a noise with. There was nothing in the room full stop, except an empty holdall, a folded pile of Iris's clothes, an anglepoise lamp and the heap of bedding up against the wall. She pointed to the lamp, which Iris had angled to make the light in the room soothing. Iris always was good at doing atmospheric things like that.

Did you bring the lamp with you? she said.

Artie's girl gave me it from a box in the barn, Iris said. It's yours. It seems you had nothing to lose but your chainstores. And now you've lost them. You're a free woman at last.

231

Those lamps aren't free, she said. They sold, when they were selling, for top price £255. Cost me £25 each.

Oh well done, Iris said.

What've you really been doing? Sophia said. Or have you taken idealistic retirement now?

I've been in Greece, Iris said. I came home three weeks ago. I'm going back in January.

Holiday? Sophia said. Second home?

Yeah, that's right, Iris said. Tell your friends that. Tell them to come too. We're all having a fabulous time. Thousands of holidaymakers arriving every day from Syria, Afghanistan, Iraq, for city-break holidays in Turkey and Greece. And the people from Yemen who've nothing to eat, they head for their holidays into Africa, where there's loads to go round for everybody especially in the countries where people are already starving, though the more sub-Saharan holidaymakers tend to head for Italy and Spain, also popular resorts with the people running away from Libya. A lot of my old friends are over in Greece, your friends'll be interested in that. I'll get together a list of names for you if you like. Tell your friends it helps if you've had a bit of experience in how to put together out of nothing a place for people to live in or sleep. Tell them a lot of new young people, energetic young people, people they'll be keen to have on their files, are there too.

None of my friends would be in the least interested in any of this, Sophia said.

Tell your friends from me, Iris said, what it's like there. Tell them people are in a very bad way. Tell them about people who've got nothing. Tell them about people risking their lives, about people whose lives are all they've got left. Tell them about what torture does to a life, what it does to a language, how it makes people unable to dare to explain to themselves, never mind to other people, what's happened to them. Tell them what loss is. Tell them, especially, about the small children who arrive there. I mean small. I mean hundreds of children. Five and six and seven years old.

Iris said it with her usual calm.

And when you've done telling them that, she said, tell them what it's like to come back here, when you're a citizen of the world who's been working with all the other citizens of the world, to be told you're a citizen of nowhere, to hear that the world's been equated with nowhere by a British Prime Minister. Ask them what kind of vicar, what kind of church, brings a child up to think that words like *very* and *hostile* and *environment* and *refugees* can ever go together in any response to what happens to people in the real world. Ask your friends in their high places that. Tell them I want to know.

I have never told anyone anything, Sophia said.

Oh, but I want you to, Iris said. Not that your old

friends are that powerful any more. But maybe you've got new friends among the new financial lobbyists. Never mind if you don't, tell your old friends all this from me anyway, I'm fond of them after all the years, fond of all their well-meaning old-fashioned ways.

Then she pointed at the ceiling above the window on the right.

That's where the birds originally got in, through the rafters, she said. There were a lot of missing slates and the floor of the loft had given way I think long before we even moved in here. That's where the birds came in and out, they were pigeons, no, they're called collared doves, they had their families here, several families over the years, I remember there were quite a lot of birds in here at one point. They made a lovely soft sound. We gave them a box full of straw to nest in but they brought their own twigs and took bits of the straw and wove them together, built nests up in the rafters and only used this room when it was rainy or cold. They mate for life, you know, those birds.

I think you'll find that's a myth, Sophia said.

We had swifts, too, under the eaves on the other side of the house. The same ones came back every year.

That sounds like a myth too, Sophia said.

Are there swifts now? Iris said. Did you have them this summer?

I've no idea, Sophia said.

You'd know if you'd swifts, Iris said. They make that high sound. I hope they're not gone. I used to lie on the grass at the back watching them teaching their young.

Iris held her arm up in the air. She did this for Sophia to come under it. Sophia gave in. She came under the arm, put her head on Iris's chest.

I hate you, Sophia said into Iris.

Iris blew hot breath into the hair on the top of Sophia's head.

I hate you too, she said.

Sophia closed her eyes.

I've never told anyone anything, she said. You're wrong about that.

I believe you, Iris said.

Nothing very important or true anyway, Sophia said.

Iris laughed.

Because Sophia's head was on Iris's chest the laugh went physically through Sophia.

Then Iris said,

Do you want to sleep in here too? There's room.

Sophia nodded against Iris.

The floor's hard, Iris said. You're a bit thin for it. I presume you're not eating again. But there's two duvets. We can use one for padding.

Iris sorted the bedding. Sophia settled into it

next to her sister. Her sister reached to switch the lamp off.

Sweet dreams, Iris said.

Sweet dreams, Sophia said.

The extraordinary way in which the Zeiss projector compresses time makes it a veritable time machine. It is the middle of the night a couple of days after Sophia's school class has been taken to London to see some historic sights, learn about royal beheadings and visit a Planetarium that opened last year, the first Planetarium in the Commonwealth. It has been built on top of the bomb damage done to Madame Tussaud's in the Blitz; a man told them in the brand new foyer that the Planetarium has been built on the crater where the first bomb to weigh 1,000 lbs fell on the city.

The whole pageant of the heavens is speeded up as if by magic; the appearances of a day, a month, a year, pass by in a matter of minutes, it says in the programme she brought home. *The centuries can be rolled back until we stand in Palestine at the time of the Nativity and witness 'The Star of Bethlehem'. We can share the excitement of Galileo Galilei when in 1610 he swept the heavens for the first time with a telescope. We can anticipate the appearance of the heavens when near the end of this century Halley's comet next returns to the vicinity of the sun.*

Sophia is thirteen. Tonight she is unable to sleep. The thing she couldn't stop thinking about when she was sitting under the dome, under the pretend night sky produced by the projector shaped like a giant insect, and the thing she can't not think about right now in bed, so much so that she's been turning over and over and the sheets have pulled out both on top and underneath, is the smallness of the capsule they put the dog into in Russia a couple of years ago which they then catapulted into the so-called heavens.

The dog died in space after a week of orbiting the earth. It died painlessly. It said so in the paper. Inside the capsule in the photo in the paper it didn't look like the dog had room even to stand up, or move much at all, never mind turn round like dogs do before they lie down, what mother calls their ancient habit, making their bed to lie in it, from the years when dogs slept in long grasses and would turn and turn to flatten the grass.

What will it have been like, the glass thing in front of the dog closing and the dog not knowing what was happening to it and the capsule hitting the sky then going beyond gravity and the dog still not knowing?

Gravity's what we have so that we *don't* fly off the surface of the earth.

Gravity, graveness.

It is like there is now a dome over Sophia's head

and brain and consciousness and in it life is being flung about unknowing in what's called space.

Why aren't you eating? mother said tonight at supper.

I cannot eat, she said, for thinking about the graveness of the life of the small dog.

What small dog? mother said.

The little Russian dog that died, she said. The one they sent into space.

But that was years ago, father said.

Then a minute later he said:

look, she's crying now. Come on, girl. It was only a dog.

She *is* very sensitive, mother said shaking her head because sensitivity is not a good thing.

Leave her sensitivity alone, Iris said. It takes serious talent, to be as sensitive as Soph is.

Iris is asleep in the other bed.

Iris is supposed to be going to secretarial school to learn to have a useful career for the years before she gets married. But letters have been coming from the secretarial school saying she's been *consistently absent and has not been attending*. Tautology, Iris said when the one saying those things came. Another came today. When father waved it over the dinner table at Iris, Iris took it, read it, pointed out first a mistake in spelling and then an inconsistency in marginal spacing, both of which proved, she said, that she knew more than they knew at secretarial college and therefore no longer needed attend.

The little Russian dog had had a clever face in the photos from when it was still alive. Laika. But Sophia has to be less sensitive. She has to pull herself together. She pulls the sheet up over her eyes. The planets are there thousands of miles above her head whether she hides her eyes or not and floating between them and the earth in a vehicle as thin as a tin can there's life itself and what's written all over its face is pure blind trust.

Sophia turns over.

She turns over again.

She can see with the light from the street lamp under the curtain that the alarm clock reads 4am.

She can see Iris two foot away from her bed in her own bed and a thousand miles away in sleep.

Sophia gets out of her ruined bed. She kneels down next to Iris's head.

What? Iris says.

She says it blurredly.

Can you what? Sure you can.

She holds open the covers. Sophia climbs in, into the warm. She puts her head on Iris's shoulder touching Iris's head. She lies in the smell of Iris which is a mix of biscuit and perfume.

Safe, Iris says.

Then it's years later, it's more than three decades later. The world has turned and turned and turned.

The moon has had people walking on it. The earth is surrounded with floating space debris, space junk and satellites, and something has woken Sophia in the middle of the night.

She puts on the light. It's Arthur. He is seven years old. He's home for Christmas. He's in tears.

I have tried to be grown up about it, he says. But I couldn't make it not be frightening and I am definitely frightened. Which is why I came.

What could possibly be so frightening? Sophia says. Nothing's as frightening as all that. Come here.

Arthur has had a nightmare. He sits on the bed. He was running through a field of corn. It was a beautiful sunny day. Then halfway across the field he realized that he and all the other children running through the field had been poisoned just by breathing in and out and getting on their skin the chemicals that the farmers have used to spray the corn, and that though it was still a sunny day and the corn was still a lovely yellow colour they were all going to die, of illness.

I woke up and I couldn't breathe, Arthur says.

Christ almighty. An Iris nightmare.

Sophia gets up. She picks Arthur up. She tucks him into her bed. She sits on the side of the bed next to him.

Now, she says. Listen. You've got to stop believing all the lies about the world being poisoned. And the bombs. And the chemicals. Because none of it is true.

Isn't it? Arthur says.

No, Sophia says. Because why would the people who do things in the world want anything but the *best* for the world?

But they do spray it with stuff, Arthur said. They do spray. I've seen them.

Yes, but, Sophia says. But. That spraying is, it's what we do to make it safe, to eat it, what's growing in the fields. The things they spray the corn with gets rid of the insects and bugs and bacteria that would ruin it otherwise, and makes the weeds that would choke it die down to let the farmers harvest it without wasting any.

Do the insects die? Arthur says.

Yes. But that's a good thing, Sophia says.

Could they not just lift them off and take them to a different field where they don't mind what they eat? Arthur says.

They're just insects, Sophia says.

Some insects are beautiful, Arthur says. Some are important.

Yes, but you don't want insects in your cornflakes, Sophia says.

Yes, but do they have to die? Arthur says.

You don't want insects in your bread, Sophia says. You don't want germs in your wheatgerm.

Arthur laughs.

Wheatgerm germs, he says.

I'll tell you what you do want, she says.

What? he says.

You want a hot chocolate. Don't you?

Yes, Arthur says. I do want that, thank you.

And then I'll tell you a story, she says. Yes?

What kind of a story? Arthur says.

A true story, Sophia says. A Christmas story.

Arthur frowns.

Then we'll play a guessing game, she says. Where you try and guess what it is you're going to get for Christmas.

Arthur nods.

Okay then, Sophia says. I'll be back in a minute. Will you be okay by yourself for just a minute?

I think so, Arthur says. If it's no longer than a single minute.

Well, you'd better be, Sophia says. Because I can't make a hot chocolate unless I'm down in the kitchen for the time it takes to make it, can I?

No, Arthur says. I suppose not.

And that might be a little longer than a single minute, but I'll be back as soon as it's made, she says. Okay?

Arthur nods.

Sophia goes downstairs.

Christ almighty. Ten past four in the morning.

She stands in the kitchen and shakes her head.

The child. So sensitive that he literally radiates

sensitivity. She herself feels physically terrible, bombarded by transference aches, every time she is anywhere near him and his sensitivity. And Christ. The Iris nightmares. She hasn't had the Iris nightmares herself for years, the ones with the tower of cloud in the distance, the flash of light, the waiting in the nondescript building with your heart going mad in your chest for the impact then the blindness that means your eyes have melted and are running down your face.

She takes a deep breath in.

She breathes it out as a sigh.

She mixes drinking-chocolate paste with milk then fills the mug with boiling water like they used to do when she was a kid, when she and Iris were kids and you weren't to use up all the milk.

Then?

It's almost a decade after that.

It's not long before her father dies.

Sophia is on the phone to him; he has called her at the office number. It is quite rare for him to do such a thing so it must surely be important. But no, it isn't important and her father has had her hauled out of the worldwide strategy video conference-call that's been set up for weeks.

The dog, he says. The Russian dog.

Yes, there *was* a dog, wasn't there? Sophia says. But I'm unable to talk right now. Can we speak later?

He's phoned, he says, because he thought she'd like to hear that the truth's just finally come out, that the poor dog that died up there more than forty years ago didn't have to circle the earth in that tin can for a whole week before it died. No. Lucky for that dog, it died only a few hours after they blasted it into space. Seven hours at the most is all it suffered for.

Right, Sophia says. And do you need anything? If you do, just tell Jeanette, I'll put you through to Jeanette and you can tell her if there's anything.

Her father is saying he has never forgotten how much it mattered to her and that he's phoned her because he thought she'd like to know what he's just read, today, in today's paper –

she can hear him shaking the paper about down the phone to get to the right page –

that the Russian scientists who'd taken that little stray dog off the streets, pretty little thing, friendly, intelligent, you can see it in the photos, bright little thing, and put her in the capsule for the experiment – which became a rush job in any case because the old bald Khrushchev was being vain and had wanted the firing of the dog into space to be a publicity stunt to celebrate something or other on a certain date, though the scientists doing the experiments with the dog weren't ready – anyway these scientists, the very men who did it, had finally revealed the truth that's been being lied about for all these years, that the little dog had died in the severe heat levels only a few hours after being fired up there, that the dog had never been expected to survive in any case, in fact they'd known it would die, they'd made the decision that it would die, before they sent it up there, and they'd just publicly said for the first time they were sorry.

Thought you'd like to know. Thought you'd appreciate knowing, this above all. That they wished now they'd never done it, never done it at all, to the dog, her father says. And, that's, well, as your mother'd say, life —

Lovely story, Sophia says. Got to go. Call you later this eve.

— time for you,

she can hear his far voice smaller and further away as she stretches over, pushes the PA button, replaces the receiver.

Burnt butter smell all through the house, middle of the night.

Sophia got up without waking her sister who was the same deep sleep snorer she'd always been.

Hi, Charlotte said.

Sophia sat down at the kitchen table.

We have to stop meeting like this, she said.

I like it. Why do we have to stop? Charlotte said.

No, I don't mean it literally. It's not literal. It's a joke. An English cliché, Sophia said. But what I don't understand, myself, Charlotte, is how you know about Shakespeare but aren't familiar with such a common cliché.

Which common cliché? Charlotte said.

What I just said. We have to stop meeting like this, Sophia said.

But I like our meeting like this, Charlotte said.

Oh very funny, Sophia said.

And don't call me Charlotte, call me Lux, she said.

I've only just got used to not calling you your full name inside my head, Sophia said. I can't call you a name that isn't yours.

You've been calling me a name that isn't mine since I met you, Charlotte said. We have to stop meeting like *that*.

Why do we? Sophia said. Since whoever you are to yourself, you are Charlotte to me. That's my view.

I'm not Charlotte, I'm Lux, Charlotte said. Who I am to myself is what in the language of English cliché is called a clever clogs egghead smartypants brainiac nerd, who started a university course here three years ago but ran out of money and now can't afford to complete it. I'm from Croatia. By which I mean I was born there. My family moved to Canada, I was quite small. It was far, but not far enough. There is a problem. The problem is, my family is war-wounded however far away we go.

Nobody in our close family died in the war, nobody was physically wounded in it, I wasn't even born till after it. But we were wounded, I was wounded, all the same. And I love my family, I love them, but when I'm with them, my wounds reopen. So I can't live with them. I can't be with them. So I came here. But my family haven't much money, and I ran out of money. And now I can't get a good job because nobody knows if I'll still be able to be here this time next year or when they'll decide we have to go. So I'm keeping myself below the radar, which is how by chance I happened to meet your son, and the truth is, your son happens to be paying me a good amount, cash in hand, to accompany him here so he won't feel bad about not being able to come here with his girlfriend, Charlotte, who he's had a fight with. With whom he's had a fight. Less informal, but more grammatically correct. You see, my English is excellent. Though it's true, I'm not up on all the clichés. And it's my view, Mrs Cleves, since we get to live by our views in your kitchen this evening, that I dislike our meetings happening, yours and mine I mean, when I'm the only person eating something. So I'd like to rectify this. Is there anything I can make you, to eat, right now? Anything you'd like?

To tell you the truth, Sophia said. I am actually feeling a little like eating something right now.

An excellent truth. What do you feel like eating?

the Croatian woman (no, more of a girl really, Sophia decided) said.

I don't precisely know what I want, Sophia said.

The girl went to the fridge. She took out a cantaloupe, cut it open and spooned out its seeds.

Would you like me to cut it into small chunks or would you like to eat it like this? she said holding up one of the cut halves. Which is one of the reasons I like this kind of melon. It is a fruit that comes complete with its own bowl, already in the bowl of itself.

You remind me of someone, Sophia said.

Is her name Charlotte? the girl said.

Ha, Sophia said.

She picked up the spoon.

Half a small melon later she put down the spoon and said:

I'd like to tell you a little about my son's father.

I'd like that, the girl said.

She sat down at the table and put her head on her hands to listen.

The love of my life, Sophia said. There really is such a thing. Though I spent almost no time with him, just one night in the dead of winter, then some years later half a week in the dead of summer.

Why did you spend so little time? the girl said.

It's just how it was, Sophia said.

Ah, the girl said. How it was. I know about that.

It was Christmas Day night, Sophia said. I was

staying in this same house we're in right now, with my sister and some of her colleagues. They were living here then, a great gang of them. I was in my early thirties, my mother had died not long before. I went for a walk, down the path, the same path, to where the main gate is now; there wasn't a gate there then, it was just an opening off the roadside with a sign on it saying the name of the house, and I went off for a walk in the dark, I didn't like the people my sister was living with, I was thinking, I'll get murdered, I'll get attacked, I'll get lost and it'll serve her, serve them all, right.

And I was walking along with my head down thinking these ridiculous thoughts and I literally walked into a man, in the dark.

He was staying with some people who lived close by. He'd come out for a walk, he said, because he was sad.

There'd been a sea storm, a Danish ship that went down, and I thought he might live locally and be worried about that, or about local people out in the rescue boats. He said he didn't know about the drowned people or the lifeboats. He was sad because he'd heard on the news that Chaplin had just died.

Who? the girl said.

Charlie Chaplin. He was a very famous film star in the silent days, Sophia said.

Oh, I know. With the big feet, the girl said. The

249

big shoes. The funny one. There's a statue in my home city.

So we were both sad about something, Sophia said. We went for a walk, we walked to the village. He went up the steps of a house and took the Christmas wreath off the front door and he held it up and he said, I am going to use this as my picture frame for tonight, and he looked back at me through it, and he said, oh yes. Yes, that's right. So I took the wreath, it was made of holly. And I looked through it and I *saw* him. I mean I saw *him*.

We took it with us to sit under this tree and we looked at everything through it all night.

Then after we said good night, good morning, we swapped addresses, and this was well before email, Charlotte, or finding people on Google, and in those days people lost touch a lot more. Which wasn't as bad a thing as you might think. Not that I wanted to lose touch with this man, I liked him, he interested me. But not long after that night I lost my purse, I left it in a taxi, and his address was folded inside it. And he was never in touch with me. So we didn't see each other again, not for years. Eight years.

Then I was walking along a London street one day, I was a different person really by then. But the man who'd never written to me, I saw him, we caught each other's eye when we walked past each other on the street. And we were so happy to see each other again that we made a plan, we planned to go to Paris for a week. And we did go to Paris.

But it wasn't right, not for me. I knew for sure there in Paris. And I was too busy for mistakes and far too busy for an improvised life by then.

It was Paris we went to because he wanted to see pictures, we went to the famous museums and galleries. In fact, he'd been here that Christmas at all because he was interested in an artist, a sculptor who lived quite near here. I mean, she was dead, she'd died some time before, but he'd come because he liked what she made so much and he'd wanted to see where she'd lived. He had a piece of her sculpture at his house, I saw it. Really it was just two round stones. But they were strikingly beautiful stones. The sculpture was in two pieces, I mean. They were meant to fit together.

But we didn't fit, he and I.

He thought it was because he was too old. He *was* older, and compared to the age I was I did think he was ancient. He was in his sixties then. Well, now I know that your sixties feel the same as all the other ages, and your seventies. You never stop being yourself on the inside, whatever age people think you are by looking at you from the outside.

And in truth, it wasn't him, it was me who was too old for him. I couldn't see a life with him. Too little in common. Not even remotely possible. I knew quite soon, very practical things meant it wouldn't be possible. Though even in that short time he taught me a great deal, he knew a great deal about all sorts of things, about art –

About your son? the girl said.

Pictures, paintings, Sophia said. I mean, I knew about Monet and Renoir, well, everybody who knew anything did. I didn't know much about the sculptor who'd lived here, I know a bit more about her now. In fact I know a lovely story I keep wishing I could tell him, about her, I read it in a paper last year, it's a story he'd have loved.

And he's dead now, the girl said.

He must be, she said. I'm old now and he was old then.

And this was Godfrey Gable, the girl said. The cut-out in the barn. But you already know he's no longer alive.

Oh dear God, no, Sophia said. I'm not talking about Godfrey.

She laughed.

Sleep with Ray! I'd never have slept with Ray. I can see him killing himself laughing in heaven at the very thought. Oh dear no. We weren't, it wasn't, like that.

So, the girl said. And you're telling me this because?

At the point at which I met Ray, Godfrey Gable is the name under which Ray worked, Sophia said, I was about to become a single mother. I wanted to keep working. He was a man who needed a family. His support protected us both and left us both free. It was a very good arrangement. I'll be forever grateful to Ray. And to Godfrey.

But, the girl said. I think this is a secret thing you're telling me.

It is sometimes easier to talk to a stranger, Sophia said.

A true cliché if ever there was one, the girl said.

It is also important in life to keep some things to yourself, Sophia said. And Arthur was my business. Nobody else's.

Like the things you buy and sell? the girl said.

Not that kind of business, Sophia said.

So now I know something intimate about your son, the girl said, about his father, which your son, I think, doesn't himself know.

Yes, Sophia said.

So. What would you like me to do with this knowledge? the girl said. Do you want me to tell him?

I don't know why I've told you, Sophia said. Perhaps because of what you told me about wounds, and about families. But no. I don't want you to tell anyone.

Then I won't, the girl said.

For one thing, the love of my life had a history to which I could never have reconciled my own family,

Sophia said. For another, I didn't want his history to be my son's inheritance.

But it's your son's history whether you want it to be or not, the girl said.

My son knows nothing about it, Sophia said. Therefore he has inherited none of it.

The girl shook her head.

Wrong, she said.

It is you who are wrong about this, Sophia said. You're young.

And what about the love? the girl said. You gave it up. The love of your life.

That was easy, Sophia said. The love of my life made my life like, like, I don't know. Like a double decker bus whose steering has gone wrong.

You couldn't keep control of it, the girl said.

You turn the wheel one way and the vehicle goes quite another, Sophia said.

The girl laughed.

You took back control of your bus routes, she said.

Then the girl put a side dish of bread with some slices of cheese on it next to Sophia.

Tell me the story instead, she said.

What story? Sophia said. There's no more story. That's it over. The end.

No, I mean the story you want to tell Art's real father but can't, the girl said.

Oh, Sophia said. That story. Oh yes. He'd have

loved it. The serendipity of it. But no. I won't, if you don't mind. That story's private.

She picked up a piece of bread and put some cheese on it.

She ate it.

She picked up another.

(Here's that story anyway that Sophia'd have liked to be able to tell the man she believed was probably now long dead, her son's father, the love of her life:

When the twentieth century artist and sculptor Barbara Hepworth was a young girl, her family, who lived in an industrial town in the north of England, used to go every year for their summer holidays to stay in a coastal village in Yorkshire. Hepworth loved it there. The people who write about her life say it's one of the reasons she felt so at home in Cornwall later in her life, that she liked this coast so much.

She loved being between land and sea. She loved being on the edge. She loved being so close to the elements and she loved the elements being so unpredictable and wild. She was quite a wild and willed girl herself, apparently, the kind of girl who'd made a point of refusing to wave her hat in the air like everybody else did to celebrate the declaration of the end of the First World War, because of all the war dead layered deep under any celebration.

She was already determined to be an artist, had made this clear to her parents, and would be going to art college in Leeds at the age of sixteen then off to London soon after. So she was very at home in a place in which a lot of artists summered, a place of striking light.

One of the summer artists, a painter in her middle years who took a house there herself every summer, was unusually famous and established for an artist who happened to be a woman, in fact she was a painter of landscapes and portraits so renowned that there's practically no municipal collection in the United Kingdom that doesn't (or didn't, given that so many collections are now sold off) have something by her in it.

Her name was Ethel Walker.

Nobody much remembers now who Ethel Walker was except the specialist art historians, and not very many of them know that much about her either.

Anyway, nearly a hundred years later, an art collector in America was surfing on eBay and he saw a quite good painting called something like Portrait of a Young Lady. It wasn't very expensive so he bought it.

When it arrived at his home and he unpacked it, it was a fetching picture of a girl in a blue dress. She looked intelligent. Even her hands looked intelligent.

On the back it said: Portrait of Miss Barbara Hepworth.

He wondered if she was by chance anything to do with Hepworth, or the gallery called the Hepworth Wakefield in the north of England.

He wrote to them to ask them and to ask if they'd like to see the painting.

Then he gave them the painting.

It's now at the Hepworth Wakefield.

And that's life and time for you.)

I'm staying with people here for the Christmas holidays, Sophia says.

Me too, the man says. Over there, the farmhouse. I came out to get some air.

Mine live up the path, Sophia says.

The man shines his torch on the sign at the roadside.

Chei Bres, the man says.

I also needed some air, Sophia says.

What does it mean? the man says.

I haven't a clue, Sophia says.

The people I'm staying with have children called Cornwall and Devon, the man says. And believe me, I've had enough of Cornwall and Devon. Not that I don't like Cornwall and Devon, I do, very much, and their parents, but it's been Christmas Day all day and I need a break from what we'll politely call the richness of Christmas tradition.

Because anyway, I'm sad. Chaplin just died, did you know? And the people I'm staying with are not appreciators of Chaplin.

The old silent film star? Sophia says.

You know his films? the man said.

No, not really, Sophia says. I thought he was funny when I was little.

The film star, the man says. The tramp. The wanderer. The first modern hero. The outcast who got people all over the world to laugh out loud together at the same things at the same time. I thought I'd go for a walk, down to the village. Away from the Micronauts and the new Yamaha Electone E-70. Don't get me wrong. I like music. Songs are my life. But Somewhere My Love performed by an eight year old for the 51st time means it's time for me to go for a walk.

They've been showing Elvis's films on TV this year now that he's dead, Sophia says. Maybe Charlie Chaplin'll be next year's Christmas film season.

Sweet Elvis in his leathers, the man says.

It is not the kind of thing a man usually says.

A blue blue Christmas without him, he says. He had some very fine songs. And dead. Young as a circus parade.

Well, in his forties, Sophia says.

The man laughs a little.

It's a line from a song, he says, the circus parade

thing. From Roustabout, the film about the fairground. The world's a clown with its nose painted red. Wonderful World. That's the name of the song.

I'm staying with people who're intent on saving the world, Sophia says. But our mother, I mean my mother, she died this year, she's dead. I'm finding it hard to care about the wonderful world per se.

Ah, the man says. I'm very sorry. For your loss.

Thank you, Sophia says.

Him saying it makes her cry. He won't see that she is crying; it is dark here. She steadies her voice.

And our father has gone abroad, Christmas with our relatives, New Zealand, she says. I have work and couldn't go. Which is why I'm here at all. But I'll know to spend next Christmas by myself.

Remind me next Christmas to do the same, the man says. Meanwhile. Let's get through this Christmas. Would you like to walk with me to the village? It's not far.

He has a nice voice in the dark. She says yes.

He looks nice too, when they get to streetlight.

He is not her usual type. He is older, maybe closer to her father's age. He is wearing very nice clothes, well cut. His shirt looks expensive. He must have money.

There's nobody about. It's not cold, though it's

quite windy. They step over a little fence and cross a green in the middle of the village. There's a wooden bench constructed in a circle round a tree whose trunk is so thick, the man says, that he thinks it must be at least Elizabethan.

He dries the bench for her with his handkerchief. They sit back against the trunk of the tree. The tree is so wide that they're completely out of the wind.

She can feel the ridges in its bark through her coat.

Are you warm enough? he says.

Too mild down here for winter, he says. I keep wishing snow would fall in its little icy chips off that old ice block in the sky.

The thing which most preoccupies me these days is, he says. How can men and women lead creative lives?

He tells her about Charlie Chaplin's father singing songs about pretty girls in the music halls and dying young and a drunkard, and Chaplin's mother singing songs in the halls too and growing madder and madder till she was too far out of her mind to work, and how Chaplin went on stage instead of his mother one night though he was still a very small child, because he knew the words of the song his mother'd been singing and his mother, there on the same stage, was staring into space as if she'd forgotten them or forgotten where and who she was, so the child Chaplin sang the song and did

260

a dance and the crowd who'd been booing his mother showered him with pennies and applause.

He hated Christmas, he says. No wonder he died at Christmas. When he was a child and was in a home for orphans, when his mother was in the asylum, the man in charge gave all the boys an apple for their Christmas except him, and this man said to him, you can't have one, Charlie, because you keep the boys awake telling them your stories. After that, he was always looking for it, always knowing he'd be denied it. He called it the red apple of happiness.

What a sad thing to know, she says. To have to know.

He apologizes for passing on a sadness.

He blames his own sadnesses.

He tells her how the boy Chaplin also played a cat in a pantomime at the Hippodrome in London, when the Hippodrome was a new theatre and had a pit which could fill with water, and all the dancing girls, dressed in armour like knights of old, would dance into the water till they disappeared under its surface, and how there was a clown who'd come out after they did and sit on the edge of the pool of water with a fishing rod using diamond necklaces for bait to try to catch a chorus girl.

He describes a picture to her by the poet William Blake, where two lovers in Dante's writing, which she has not yet read but will now, are meeting in heaven, and how there's a woman in the scene whose pigtails are like braids made of happy infant souls, how the angels in the picture have wings covered in open eyes, and how a woman who's meant to be hope personified stands off to the side, she's wearing a green dress, she's smiling and throwing her hands up skywards.

He flings his own arms in the air under the tree to show her hope.

She laughs out loud.

Beautiful happy hope, he says.

They shelter in the wooden hut at the village bus stop. He holds up the holly wreath he stole off the door again. He looks at her through it. He is like no man she has ever spent time with. He seems not in the least interested in the things the older men who want to talk to you are interested in.

But I'm old now, he says. You're young. You probably think I'm senile. And it's true, I tend to let fair things pass by unheeded as a threshold brook.

You tend to what? she says.

He laughs. He tells her it's Keats, not him, talking.

Then tell Keats not to be so stupid, she says.

Some people walk past the green. Merry Christmas! the people shout. Merry Christmas! they both shout back. The face of the church clock says half past two. I'd better get back to my west countries, he says. They'll have locked the door on me.

They return the holly wreath to its rightful door. This is the kind of man he is. He walks her home in the wind to the start of the path off the road, Chei Bres. When they get there he insists. He walks her all the way to the house up the dark tree-rooted path.

Big house, he says when they get there. My goodness.

The lights are still on. People are up, of course they are. They sleep in the daytime here like vampires.

It won't be locked, she says. They're not the door-locking type.

How hospitable, he says.

One day, she says. I'll own this house. I'm going to buy it one day.

You will, he says. You are.

He kisses her on the mouth.

If they've locked up at your place, come back here, she says. You can sleep here.

Thank you, he says. It's most kind.

He wishes her a happy Christmas.

When she can't hear his going away any more she opens the door and goes in. She stands at the bottom of the stairs, considers going straight up to bed. But she changes her mind. He might come back. She'll wait up, half an hour. She goes through to the kitchen. It's full of dope smoke and dopey people, someone strumming a guitar, one of the girls doing dishes, quarter past three in the morning.

Nobody asks her where she's been.

Probably nobody noticed she'd even gone out.

She puts the kettle on to make a hot water bottle.

I met a man, she tells Iris.

Sing hallelujah, Iris says.

He's here in this part of the world because he really likes the artist who made the stones with the holes in them and lived over in St Ives, is St Ives near here? she says. He was sad. Charlie Chaplin's died today. I mean yesterday. Christmas Day.

Chaplin's died?

The news goes round the table.

Aw.

Shafted by America.

Good comrade.

Great Dictator, Iris says. Great film.

Iris starts talking about the new dictatorship of the media and the new feudal system the tabloids are milking, the readers the slaves of their propaganda.

Sophia yawns.

One of the men, a man whose shirt collar is filthy, whose hair is long and stringy and whose baldspot makes him look a bit like a medieval monk, tells her Hepworth is the name of the artist who lived near here and that she was anti nuclear. Sophia rolls her eyes to herself. I bet they say that about everyone, she thinks. Especially the dead. I bet they enlist all the great and good to their side as soon as they can't speak for themselves about what it is they believe.

I honestly doubt it since anybody with any powers of logic and understanding knows we need nuclear weapons, she says out loud.

The whole room turns towards her like in that unnatural way owls can move their heads right round without moving the rest of their bodies.

It's obvious, she says. We need them to stop the other countries with nuclear weapons attacking us with their nuclear weapons. Simple maths, comrades.

She feels brave and witty for the first time in months. Calling them comrades to their faces.

And I don't know how you'd prove, anyway, she says, that this artist who's now dead and can't speak for herself was anti nuclear while she was alive.

No one can argue otherwise with her. All they can say is, you're wrong about that. She just was, they say. You can see it in her work, they say.

They bring up other important people. One woman even brings up Lord Mountbatten. As if Lord Mountbatten, a military man himself, would be anti nuclear. A military royal would never be so stupid and short sighted and blind.

She'll learn, Iris says. Give her time.

Sophia purses her just-kissed lips.

She fills her bottle. She puts the kettle back on the hob. One of the queue of people waiting for a warm drink shakes that kettle so everyone can hear how little water's left in it.

She doesn't care.

She has unexpectedly had one of the best Christmases ever.

She has met a man who knows about Dante, Blake and Keats, who can speak like words are themselves magic things, and who apologized to her, who sensed that she has feelings and who bowed to them, who has looked at her through holly leaves and described all sorts of things to her, described art, poems, theatre, described the green dress of hope.

She has been sitting with her back against an Elizabethan tree. Her head is full of girls in suits of armour dancing down into water till it's over their heads, girls under the surface waiting for the flash of light on the fisherman's hook.

It was still early enough to be dark out. The foreign girl had gone back out to the barn to sleep. Arthur was asleep there too. Her sister was asleep in the top of the house.

Sophia went to her room. She closed the door. She opened her wardrobe. She took out the shoes, pair by pair, from the floor of the wardrobe. This took quite some time. She liked shoes. She had a lot of shoes. She was a shoe person.

She lifted the wardrobe's flooring.

She took out the stone with both hands. It was weighty. In the fade from the dark to the morning light it looked fluently veined. It was pale red/brown, very like the material they used to line the upper walls of the Pantheon in Rome. Sophia had seen it, an ancient church where the Renaissance artist Raphael's remains were kept in a stone box over at one side, with a thousand people flashing their phones and cameras at the box all day from the moment they opened the doors of the place, doors so tall and heavy that they'd always open with a forced serenity, it'd be impossible for them not to, in a building that's almost always too busy, almost always a mess of people and happens also to be a mess of overdone decor on its lower level in Sophia's opinion.

But as the eye rises, and the building itself rises, everything simplifies till there's nothing but near-plain relief-carved squares-inside-squares of clean stone. Then at the top and the heart of the dome there's a round opening like a vision, the open air itself, the light, nothing but sky for a roof.

Pantheon.

All the gods.

What was it again, in the old pretty poem, that melts away, like snow in May, as if there were no

such cold thing? It was true that stone was cold,
until you warmed it. This ball of stone would have
come from a warm country originally, would it?
She'd heard on the radio someone talking once
about a marble-like stone from the north of
England and the woman on the radio said that
stones had scents and that the northern stone
sometimes gave off the smell of decay because it
was composed partly of ancient shells of once-living
creatures which decomposed when you broke the
stone open and they met the air again.

She raised the stone to her nose. It smelt of her
wardrobe, her own perfume.

She held it against her face.

Its skin was faultless.

Out in the early morning through the window
the light was up but there was no traffic noise, not
yet, too early. What there was instead was the
winter sound of crows with the birdsong above it,
like two weatherfronts meeting, like the coming
season getting ready midway through the old one to
make itself heard.

She put it back inside on the tissue paper. The
tissue paper was quite new; the last cushion of
tissue paper in here had been feeding a batch of
those small gold moths. She laughed whenever she
thought about that; she'd looked up into her own
clothes hanging there, then out and round the
room. Moths could eat it all if they liked. This

whole house could fall away to nothing, and when it did, at the centre of its wreckage?

The stone, beautiful, unchanged.

She replaced the floor plank then the first of the pairs of shoes, then the next and the next, and so on.

It is a balmy Tuesday in July 1985, late morning on Great Portland Street in London.

Is it you? he says. It is you!

And it's you, she says. Danny.

Sophie, he says. The address you gave me. I lost it.

I lost yours too, she says.

I put it in my pocket and the next time I looked it was gone, it just wasn't there, he says. It was terrible.

I bet Cornwall took it, she says.

You bet what? he says.

Or Devon, she says.

Oh. Ha! Ha ha, he says. You remember. Oh my goodness. You look so like you. You look even more like you than I remember. You look beautiful.

No I don't, she says. And look at you.

Older, he says.

You're the same, she says.

Given that Devon's at university now and Cornwall's been and done A levels, he says.

She laughs.

You look exactly the same, she says.

And I found out what Chei Bres means, he says.

What what means? she says.

The name of the house, he says. It's Cornish. Of course.

You speak Cornish now? she says.

Well, no, he says, just the same old German and French and Italian and I can still read a bit of the Hebrew if pressed, but Cornish I can't, no, but I looked it up, and it means House of the mind, of the head, of the psyche. Psyche's House. I looked it up back then, in 1978. I've been waiting to tell you.

Well, she says.

Well, he says.

Now you have, she says.

Yes, he says.

Thank you, she says. I can't believe you even remembered.

How could I forget? he says. Where are you off to now? Can we go for a, can you come for a coffee or something?

I've got a meeting, she says. But, oh –.

Oh, okay, he says. Well, we can, another –.

No. I mean yes. I mean, I can miss the meeting, she says.

They take a cab. His house is on the Cromwell Road, he tells her he bought it cheap in the 60s. It'll be worth a fortune now, she thinks. Its windows are huge and it's all been knocked into open plan space, bedroom above the living room, kitchen below. Its shelves are all books and art, beauty everywhere. When they have sex (and they have sex immediately, as soon as he's closed the front door) it's the best sex she has yet had. It's not like sex. It's like she's been heard, seen, paid attention to, not shagged or fucked or screwed, not like just sex – more like something she's never, something that she hasn't a name for. Something she can't put into words happens.

That sounds quite rude; see what happens with words? It's not what she means. She means words will make it less than it is, or something it isn't.

Later on her way home, as she walks down a street, there'll be words again, she'll be *dazed* with it, *blasted* by it, *made roofless like a house after a gale* by it and the *walls all down*, made *open*, maybe such a thing as *too open* because this street she'll be on, it's a pretty run-down street but it will be vibrant to her, though below her there'll be nothing but a pavement, but beautiful, the pavement, well get real, pavements aren't beautiful, and the bus shelter a beauty, buildings, scruffy, beautiful, beautiful fast food place, shockingly beautiful coin-operated launderette full of strangers whose profiles in the late evening sun are, yes, though she'll know they aren't really, but they will be, right then, unbelievably beautiful.

Now though she stretches out naked on the long

couch. She looks at the art on the walls of the place while he goes downstairs to make something to eat in the kitchen. Some of the art looks really modern. Some of it looks primitive, that stone with a hole in it like a small standing stone.

Like in the book The Owl Service, she tells him when he comes back up.

Yes, he says, and she does that, Hepworth, I think, puts the holes through what she makes, because she wants people to think about exactly what you just said, time, and ancient things, but also because she really just wants them to want to touch what she makes, you know, to be reminded about things that are quite physical, sensory, immediate, he says.

A gallery'd never allow people touching it, she says.

More's the pity, he says.

Is it worth a lot of money? she says. I mean, they, are they?

I don't know, he says. Things are always worth more after someone dies, and it's ten years now since she went. I just love it. That's what makes it worth the world.

He tells her they're sort of a mother and child pairing, the child stone the little one and the larger stone the mother. The larger stone has the hole in it and a flat place on it where the smaller stone is meant to sit.

272

He tells her the artist said that she was tired of faces and of dramas and that she wanted a universal language.

One where the world itself speaks, he says, not just us on the surface arguing the toss in all the different languages all across it.

She puts a hand out towards the stones.

Can I? she says.

Yes, he says. You have to.

She picks up the smaller rounder stone, curved like a breast, heavy. She cups it in her hands. She puts it back where it was. She fingers the hole through the larger stone. It's nothing but a circle carved through stone. But it's sort of amazing. It's unexpectedly satisfying to touch.

It would be good to be full of holes, she says. Then all the things you can't express would maybe just flow out.

What a thoughtful way to see it, he says.

She blushes at the thought that she's thoughtful.

She walks round the sculpture. It *makes* you walk round it, it makes you look through it from different sides, see different things from different positions. It's also like seeing inside and outside something at once.

She doesn't say so in case he thinks she's showing off.

It is stone, two stones is all it is and one with a hole in it.

273

She sits down again, settles back into his arms like he's an armchair.

Do you know that story, she says, about the brilliant artist and the king, and the king sends his men to get the artist to make the perfect work of art for him, and the artist draws a circle, just a circle, nothing else, but it's a perfect circle, and gives it to them and says give your king this from me?

That's an old story about the artist called Giotto, he says at her ear.

Oh bless you, she says.

I wasn't sneezing, he says. Giotto's his name.

I know, she says. I mean I know you weren't sneezing. I meant it, a blessing. I'm saying a sort of thank you.

For what? he says.

For knowing what I was talking about, she says, first of all. Then for making that story real, about a real person, not just a myth. It's a story I've known since I was little. I didn't know it was true.

I don't know that it's true, it's more probably apocryphal, he says. But what else are we? We're all apocrypha.

She tells him that scientists have just sent up into space a machine called a Giotto to take pictures of the stars and the coming comet.

Wait a minute, he says.

He goes over to the shelves by the window where

274

all the books in all their languages are. Sunlight hits his bare shoulders.

Giotto, he says.

Then he smiles.

Bless me, he says.

It ought to be really boring, someone you've just been intimate with getting up and going and getting a book off a shelf and then you having to look at it. It's the opposite. He kneels down next to the couch, opens the book.

Christmas in July, he says.

What a blue, she says.

And the red and the gold in the blue, he says. That star. Fiery ice. Ice and dust and nucleus. The Virgin's cloak would all have been blue too. It's lost its blue. There's no blue like a Giotto blue. The star was presumably brighter too, originally. Hard to imagine how it could be. The star's the star of the show. I mean comet. They think it's an early painting of Halley's comet.

It's due back, she says. Next year. I've been waiting for this comet since I was thirteen.

She looks at the page done by the artist who drew the perfect circle. There are camels in this picture that appear to be laughing with delight, though all the humans and angels look so serious, the kings with their gifts, one king kissing the feet of the infant.

She looks at how they all appear to be standing

275

balanced on a narrow cliff. She runs her finger along its edge.

Look, she says. They're in Cornwall.

He laughs.

They're actually in Padua, he says. I mean in real life. We should go and see them, see the first Giotto comet before the new Giotto sees it. Let's do that. Let's go and see it. Let's go to Italy.

Italy? she says.

Tomorrow, he says. Tonight.

I can't just go to Italy, she says.

Well, okay, he says. France, then. Let's go to Paris. Just for a day or two. I mean it. There's a few things there I'd like to see.

Paris, she says.

What do you say? he says. It's not far. It's not as far as Italy. Will you come? Will we go?

I've work, she says.

I've work too, he says.

He smiles at her.

You're a man of the moment, she says.

I am, he says. Is that a good thing?

Yes and no, she says.

They put the book down, still open.

They do the wordless thing again.

It goes all through her.

It is so good it's frightening.

She'll have to be careful, with this one, to be sure to keep her head.

On the shortest day in 1981, in the snowiest December since 1878 and on a foggy damp cold Monday morning, the people who are camped outside the main gate of the airbase wake up to the sound of bulldozers.

The earth has been flattened all round the camp. A new sewage system will be running, the military authorities have decided, right underneath the protesters.

Like hell it will.

Some of the camp members sit down on the ground in front of and behind the digger. They refuse to move.

The work stops.

The protesters tell the camp commander there will be no laying of sewage pipes.

They tell each other, privately, that they'll have to

be up a bit earlier next time not to be caught on the hop.

The number of protesters living at the camp tends to vary right now between six and twelve people, still both sexes, though soon the camp will become a women's protest only. This decision will cause a good few arguments over the months and years.

There's a blue Portakabin for urgent shelter. That won't last. It'll be dismantled and taken away not long from now.

There's a communal area made out of plastic, tarpaulin and tree branches. People come and give talks in it and it's somewhere a bit less weather-worn to sit. It won't last either.

Some local people have been kind and have made available their bathrooms to the protesters; this was crucial when the base command turned off the water main across the road. So the protesters wrote to the water authorities. The water authorities now charge them a monthly rate.

Soon the numbers of protesters will rise beyond anything imagined. The women will be threading coloured wool and ribbon through the fencewire and across between the gates in intricate webbing, they'll be cutting holes in the perimeter fence with wirecutters and breaking into the base almost every night then being sent to court to be charged with breaching the peace then back to the camp after fines and imprisonments and cutting the holes in the fence again.

There will soon almost always be holes in the fence, as many holes as there are new songs coined and sung by the protesters. In fact there'll be so many songs sung in the camp that writing them all down will take over a hundred pages. There's a hole in your fence, dear Major, dear Major. Then fix it, dear Private. But the women are cutting it, dear Major, dear Major. Then arrest them, dear Private. But that doesn't stop them, dear Major, dear Major. Then shoot them, dear Private. But the women are singing, dear Major, dear Major. The military and the police will soon discover that there's not much action they can take, in stopping a protest by a group of singing women, that doesn't reveal the shame and the core brutality in the action they take.

In just under two years from now the first cruise missiles will arrive.

In just under a year from now on a sleety December Sunday more than 30,000 women from all across the country, all across the world, will line up round the base fence, nine miles of fence and nine miles of people. They'll join hands in a human fence.

This will have been organized by chain letter. Embrace the base. Send this letter to ten of your friends. Ask them to send it to ten of their friends.

They think of themselves, the protesters, as wakers of sleepers.

They consider the millions of people in the world who can't see the danger as snowblind or like explorers in a polar region about to make the mistake of lying down and going to sleep in the snow; books about them afterwards will comment on how this is one of the analogies the protesters like most to use when it comes to trying to describe to the world the urgency of what they're doing.

Close your eyes and you're dead.

For now, though, it's the protest's first Christmas week (and there'll be Christmas weeks spent protesting here till all the way into the new century). The postman delivers the post. The protesters heat the water up to make him a cup of tea. He sits down to drink it on a chair that'll shortly be mashed by the bailiff's pulping machine. Right now it's still a chair.

After it's gone?

Sit on the ground.

The time will come when the military authorities will flatten this camp completely and make it impossible to rebuild it here, when they widen the road into the main gate improving access for increased military traffic.

The protesters will move slightly along from where the first camp was and settle there instead.

Back in London a few days into the new year, Art will be lying in bed in the empty flat flinching at the memory of how useless he was when Charlotte said the thing about the dream she kept having, of herself cut open at the chest with the chicken scissors.

That particular uselessness, of all his many uselessnesses, will haunt him. It will, yes, cut him open.

He will wish he'd got up from behind the screen he was looking at and crossed the room and just hugged her whenever she'd told him that dream. Just a hug, right then, would've been better than the nothing he did, the worse-than-nothing he did, the despising her because she'd felt something, because she'd tried to give it words, give it an image.

He will wish he'd been the kind of man who says, if his partner tells him something like that dream, *don't worry love, I can mend this, wait a minute*, and then knows to pretend to be a surgeon with an imaginary metaphysical needle and thread and to mime sewing up the zigzag divide. Even just the gesture of stitches.

It would at least have been a paying of attention.

What he will do, halfway through the month of January, is write Charlotte a letter in which he will tell her he'd like very much to pass over the domain, the maintenance and the workings of the Art in Nature blog to her, if she'd like it. He will write that he knows he wasn't really up to it, that he knows that she is and will be. He will write that he knows she'll be brilliant at it. He will sign off his letter with love.

He will also send an email to the SA4A Entertainment Division and ask if it will be possible to meet someone from the organization to have a chat, person to person, just generally, about the company and his role in it.

What Charlotte will do is write a very nice letter back in which she will apologize for what she did to his laptop and offer to buy him a new one. He will write back and thank her and say he'd love a new laptop. (He will be polite and resist suggesting make, model and OS.)

Within days Charlotte will have posted a blog

about how the camera eye of the drone has taken over from the crane shot as the eye of God in TV and film dramas. It'll be really good. The Art in Nature hits will start to soar. She'll follow this with a blog about the ubiquity of plastic microbeads in everything from clothes to saliva. Then she'll post a blog about sexism in parliament.

Within half an hour of sending his email to SA4A, Art will get the usual reply from the usual friendly-sounding SA4A bot addressing him in a friendly way and sending him the SA4A website link as information about contacting the SA4A Entertainment Division.

He will write back again asking if it's possible to be referred to a real person by the bot, to set up a meeting just to say a hello in person to his employers.

Within half an hour he will get the usual reply from the usual friendly-sounding SA4A bot with the website link for contacting the SA4A Entertainment Division.

He'll go to the website. He'll click on CONTACT US.

It will give him the e-address of the friendly-sounding bot with whom he's just been communicating.

Let's do the impossible now and look through a window we can't physically see through at all, given the winter condensation on the ones along the side of the barn, where Art is rolled in Lux's makeshift bed and Lux is sitting crosslegged above him on one of the stock crates.

It is Boxing Day morning, towards 10am. Art has just woken up. Lux has brought him a mug of coffee. His aunt's in the kitchen making breakfast, Lux says; she says his mother and his aunt are both in the same room and are not arguing, and no, the dining room is not full of coastline, there is no coastline to be seen anywhere in it or in the kitchen or in any of the rooms she's been in this morning.

But it was, Art says. In the room. With us. Over our heads. Like someone had cut a slice out of the coast and dipped it into the room with us, like we're the coffee and it's the biscotti. And them arguing under it and you just sitting there and none of you with any idea it was even there.

The coastline that came to dinner, she says.

He scratches his head. He rubs his thumb against his fingers. He holds his fingers out to show her.

I've still got bits of it in my hair, he says. See? I wasn't drunk. I really did see it. It really was really there.

Like you banged your head on the world, Lux says. You're like the dictionary doctor.

The what? he says.

Kicking the big stone with his foot, she says, to

prove that reality is reality and that reality physically exists. I refute it thus.

Who? Art says.

The literature doctor, she says. The man who wrote the dictionary. Johnson. Not Boris. The opposite of Boris. A man interested in the meanings of words, not one whose interests leave words meaningless.

How do you know all this stuff? he says. About books and dictionaries. Shakespeare. You know more about Shakespeare than I do.

I've got a deg, she says.

A what? he says.

The first half of a degree, she says. And I spend my days off in the library. Well. Used to. Did.

And you saw nothing? he says. You really saw nothing?

The earth didn't move for me, she says. I saw the room, and us in it. I was there. But I didn't see any coast, or land, or anything like you describe, in the room. No.

See a doctor, he says.

You see a doctor? she says.

She stands up on the box and looks all round the barn.

No, I mean I'll see one, I'll phone and get an appointment when the surgeries reopen, he says.

And that won't take long, she says sitting down again. It only takes an average of six months just now in your country to get any real help for serious mental health issues.

But I'm going mad, he says.

He cuddles back down under the duvet. He pulls it up over his head. Lux gets down off the box and sits by his feet, he can feel her sitting there. She takes his foot in her hand through the duvet and holds it. It's nice.

I said to your aunt last night, she says. After you came out here, when you were asleep. I said, Art is seeing things. And your aunt said, that's a great description of what art is.

Then your aunt said it wasn't surprising you were seeing things and that we're living in strange times. Then she told me she'd been walking through a railway station last week and she'd seen four policemen all dressed in black with machine guns and they were standing asking some old people on the concourse looking at a map if they needed any help with their directions. The old people looked really small and frail. The police looked huge, like giants, next to them. And she thought, either I'm seeing things or the world is crazy.

Then she thought to herself, but what's new? I've been seeing things in the crazy world all my life.

And I said, no, that the thing *you'd* seen had been a hallucination, not a real thing. And then she said this:

where would we be without our ability to see beyond what it is we're supposed to be seeing.

What about you? Art says from inside the duvet. Have you ever?

Coastlined? she says. Well. I'll take you on a short tour of one of my coastlines.

One of my mother's uncles was doing the family tree thing when I was about ten and he showed me my place on the map of people he'd made, I was down at the bottom. I looked at all the names above mine, going back and back in time, all the centuries that the names meant, and I thought, look at all those people over my head, real people and all related to, all a part of me, and I know nothing, absolutely nothing, about almost all of the people on that map.

And then this happened, years later, when I was seventeen, walking along a street in Toronto and I stopped and just stood there in the middle of Queen Street because the day went dark all round me even though it was the middle of the day, and I knew for the first time I was, I am, carrying on my head, like a washerwoman or a waterwoman, not just one container or basket, but hundreds of baskets all balanced on each other, full to their tops with bones, high as a skyscraper, and they were so heavy on my head and shoulders that either I was going to have to offload them or they were going to drive me down through the pavement into the ground, like that machine that workmen use to break up tarmac, and all I could think was, it's so dark I wish I had a torch, I wish I had just a box of matches, just a tiny struck match in the dark will do to be able to see where to put my feet, get a grip, so I can balance and put these things I'm carrying down and look into each basket, offer it respect, do it justice. Don't misunderstand me. I also knew they weren't there, there were no bones, no baskets, nothing on my head. But all the same. They were. There. I mean here.

Yes, Art says.

Though on the other hand, Lux says. When I spoke to your mother about what you'd seen last night, she looked annoyed and said you should snap out of it. I think your mother is one of the millions and millions of people who live every day at the finis of their terre.

But Art under the duvet doesn't hear what she's saying about his mother because he's begun to hear a rumbling sound and feel the floor pulsing under him.

Oh dear God.

He pulls the duvet off his head.

He holds his hand up to ask Lux to stop talking.

What? she says.

I think it's happening again, he says.

Is it? she says.

The air is rumbling, he says. The ground is shaking.

It is, she says. Like traffic, or an aeroplane.

Can you hear it too? he says.

She nods.

He gets up. He goes over to the door and opens it a crack. A single decker bus full of people is reversing and then jolting forward, inching its way up the path outside the barn, going up the road towards the house.

I'm seeing a bus, Art says.

I'm seeing a bus too, Lux says.

Art pulls clothes on. When they get to the house the bus is parked on the drive, its door open. Lux knocks on the bus's metal side.

I refute it bus, she says.

There's a man at the wheel holding a cigarette out of his side window as far from himself as he can.

It's a no smoking bus, the man says.

The house is full of people. There's a pile of coats and boots in the porch. There's a queue of people waiting outside the little toilet room in the hall.

A stranger is sitting in his mother's study working at his mother's computer.

Don't speak to me, the man says. I'm on FaceTime.

A woman is standing behind him looking bored. The man starts talking to somebody onscreen about map co-ordinates.

This is my husband, the woman says, and this is

the worst Christmas I've had in my life thanks very much for asking, I've just spent all Christmas night trying to get to sleep on a bus and I don't even like rare birds.

The woman introduces herself as Sheena MacCallum and says that she and her husband, their three grown-up kids and their grown-up kids' partners have all been on this bus since it left Edinburgh last night. The bus has been picking up keen birdwatchers all the way down the country. Her husband organized this bus. She herself doesn't care whether she ever or never sees a Canada warbler in her life. But her husband knew there'd be money in it as well as a possible bird sighting and decided a great deal of people *would* want to if they had the chance, even if it meant travelling at Christmas, and that they'd pay well for the experience if someone were to organize it.

And he was right, she says. What can I say? The world is full of people looking for meaning in the shape of a bird not native to this country turning up in this country after all.

Her husband winks at Art from behind FaceTime and rubs his fingers and his thumb together.

A very happy Christmas to me, Mr MacCallum says.

The woman called Sheena introduces her children to Lux. Art goes into the kitchen. People in their socks are padding about; people are sitting round the kitchen table drinking hot drinks; Iris is at the Aga frying and boiling eggs and a woman is buttering slices of toast.

Art dares to go into the dining room.

There is no coastline at all anywhere in the dining room.

Okay.

Good.

The dining table is covered in leftovers from last night's meal to which people are helping themselves. The people round it make a great fuss when they find out who Art is. People shake his hand. People thank him. They are excited to meet him. It is like they think he is some kind of a celebrity.

What did it look like? a man says. Did you get any pictures?

I didn't, Art says.

But you saw it, the man says.

Art blushes.

I –, he says.

He's about to tell them all the truth. But the man shows him a map of Cornwall with ink crosses marked all over it and says:

I know, I know. Your bird has flown. It happens to the best of us. But you *saw* it. We're keen to get a look at where you saw it anyway, if you can pinpoint it for us. Just in case. You never know your luck. Then we're meeting another group that's come down in a bus from London over at Mousehole to check the other locations.

What other locations? Art says.

We're going to check *all* the sighting locations, the maybes and the verified, the man says.

There've been verified sightings? Art says. Of a real Canada warbler?

Where've you been? the man says. It's all over the net!

Reception, Art says.

The man points out on the map where four possible sightings and three definite sightings have taken place.

He shows Art a photo on his phone, then another, and another.

It does look like a Canada warbler. And behind the Canada warbler the landscape does look like here.

It really is, Art says. My God.

And you've seen it, the man says. You're one of the lucky ones. The mythical Canada warbler, and you're one of the few people on earth to see it with their own eyes on this side of the pond.

And in any case, the man called Mr MacCallum says coming through and putting his arm round Art's shoulders, whether we're as lucky as you or not there's plenty more birds in the sea round here. I'm excited enough, myself, at getting to go to a place called Mousehole.

The woman called Sheena rolls her eyes.

I can help, Iris tells her. I have some spare Christmas spirit. Come with me.

Oh good, you're up, Arthur, his mother says. I'd like to show some of the visitors the stock in the barn before they go to the coast.

Quite a lot of people follow his mother outside.

But Art starts to worry. If he is meant to be such a nature lover, such a nature thinker, shouldn't he also be going with them on the bus to see the Canada warbler? Why isn't he more excited at the thought that he might get, really, to see a once-in-a-lifetime bird that's survived the ocean and arrived by the skin of its beak?

But this isn't what's really worrying him about the thought of the bus and the birders.

What's really worrying him is that these people on this bus from the north are off to meet a group who've come on a bus from London. And what if Lux might take it into her head to decide she'd like to ask those people from London for a lift back to London on their bus?

She will want to leave with them, surely.

It is her chance to get out of here today, to not have to wait till tomorrow.

She will have had enough of being anything to do with the unhinged life of a person who sees coastline that isn't really there, and his unhinged mother who told her she wasn't welcome.

She hasn't even had a bed to sleep in here.

He'd leave, if he were her.

He has no idea where Lux is right now. He hasn't seen her since they came back up to the house. Has she maybe already got on the bus?

The too-real bus?

He goes and looks.

She's not on the bus. Nobody is on the bus except the driver who offers him a cigarette. No, thank you, Art says. But have you a couple of matches you could spare me?

He looks upstairs in the attic, then in all the empty rooms. He looks in the dining room again and in the office. He looks out in the back garden, goes right down to the fence between the garden and the field. He comes back towards the noise of the house, looks in the lobby and finally the kitchen where Iris is standing by the sink pouring a sweet-smelling alcohol into a hipflask the woman called Sheena is holding out.

When the others off the bus see Iris doing this a murmur goes round the group and a polite queue of people holding hipflasks and plastic water bottles forms in front of Iris.

The birdwatchers stay for about half an hour more. They pick up their cameras, pull their coats and boots back on, shout their thank-yous and get back on their bus. The bus does a three point turn in the drive only hitting the side of the house twice, and rocks its way down the path between the trees with the people inside waving from the back window till they can't see the house any more.

The woman called Sheena is waving one of the anglepoise lamps from the stock in the barn in the air.

His mother, standing next to him at the door, opens her hands as the bus leaves. She shows Art the roll of banknotes.

Boxing Day sale, she says. Everything must go. Did you know your girlfriend's a natural salesperson as well as a virtuoso on the violin?

Boxing Day later afternoon; the light is gone outside, which makes it evening; the room is a winter dream of warmth. Art is dozing in a chair. Lux is sitting on the floor leaning against his legs like a girlfriend or real partner in front of the open fire in the lounge. It all almost feels like an imagined Christmas might.

His mother is talking (quite rationally) to his aunt about the programmes that used to be on all the TV channels first thing on Christmas mornings when they were small, televised live from children's wards in hospitals, as if to remind people to think of people worse off or realize how lucky they were not to be in hospital or be having to worry about a child in hospital at Christmas time.

Not that we ever watched them, his mother says. But even if we switched them off, still, somewhere at the backs of our heads, at least we thought about people in hospitals while we had our hospital-free Christmas. And there was something good in the thought.

You old Catholic, Iris says.

Well, yes and no, his mother says. Because those programmes did us all a service. They made us think of others whether we wanted to or not. Presumably they were very poor television, unless you happened to be related to someone in a hospital at Christmas time personally visited by the cameras and Michael Aspel or whoever. Then you'd be interested. Then you'd really care.

I remember father telling us, when we were small, Iris says. You're maybe too small to remember. About how his father took him, in the years after the First World War, to see the war veterans in the hospitals on Christmas Day. Maybe the ethos of those programmes comes from those post-war visits, the post-war times.

Basically, Art thinks in his half-dozing state, though nobody'd dare say it now, everybody in those wars must've been close to mad, not so much spunky Kenneth More with his flying helmet on swinging himself into the cockpit of the Spitfire even though he's had his legs amputated, more the crazy man in the film called A Canterbury Tale who goes round pouring glue into the hair on the heads of anyone female in the army.

I remember father telling me, too, Iris is saying, and it's something nobody ever talks about now. That the government after that war took to lying to huge numbers of people who'd been victims of the mustard gas attacks, and to their families, telling them that it wasn't the gas that was making them ill but that they had tuberculosis, and they did this so the state wouldn't have to pay all those wounded men and their families a war pension.

His mother snorts.

A typical Iris anti-establishment folktale if ever I heard one, she says.

Iris laughs lightly.

Not even you, Soph, with all your powers of wisdom, all your business acumen and all your natural intelligence, can make something not be true just by declaring it's not true.

You'll never stop, will you? his mother is saying. (But she is saying it fondly.) You're going to chip chip chip away at the unchippable edifice all your life. Be truthful. Don't you ever get fed up? You know it's hopeless. Your life. A work of endless futility.

Oh I'm much less ambitious these days, Iris says, now that I'm so much older, wiser, stiffer of limb. These days, since we're talking truth, I see those signs that say keep out, access forbidden, CCTV in operation, and I realize I'd be quite content just to be a bit of moss in the sun and the rain and the time passing, happy to be nothing but the moss that takes hold on the surfaces of those signs and greens itself over their words.

Since we're talking truth, Art says still with his eyes closed, I've a question for you both.

Ooh, a question, his mother says.

For us both, Iris says. Ask away, son.

He is not, his mother says. Your son.

He tells them that he has a memory of being told a story when he was very small. The story was about a boy lost in the snow at Christmas who finds himself in the underworld.

Ah, Iris says. Yes. I told you that story.

No she didn't, his mother says.

Yes I did, Iris says.

I know for sure she didn't, his mother says. Because it was me. I told you it.

You were on my knee in the Newlyn cottage, Iris says. We'd been out for a walk by the boats. You were sad because you'd never seen snow. I told you you had, but that you'd been too small to remember it. Then I told you that story.

Don't listen to her, his mother said. You were in my bed, you'd had a nightmare. I brought you up some hot chocolate. You asked me what the wrong kind of snow was, you'd heard someone say it on the TV. And I told you the story.

I sat you on my knee, Iris said, and told you it, and I remember it so specifically because I went out

298

of my way to make the child in the story neither a boy nor a girl.

He remembers it as a boy, his mother says. So it's my story he remembers. I'm sure I'll have made it a boy. Yes, I did, and I myself remember it so specifically because I wove in a lot of facts I knew you'd love, Arthur, about things like philosophers, and camera tricks, because we'd been to the Museum of the Moving Image and you'd loved it, and I put in astronomers, and the people who'd studied the shapes of snowflakes. You remember.

No, Art says. I remember going to MOMI though. And I remember someone telling me something about stars and snow.

Kepler, his mother says. *I* told you about him. I told you about Kepler and the comet and the snowflakes. *She* doesn't know who Kepler *is*.

The reason I made the hero of the story I told you, Artie, be a *child*, in other words a hero who could be a boy *or* a girl, Iris says, is because our own mother told us that story when we were little and she told it with a girl in it who melted right through the floor of the underworld in her galoshes, and I wanted you to be able to put yourself into the story if you chose to.

In her ga-what? Lux says.

Galoshes, Art says.

What a fine word, Lux says.

They're not at all exotic, don't get yourself

excited, Charlotte, his mother says. And since we're talking truth. There is no truth in this endless lie that you lived with her, Arthur. Once and for all, you never lived with her. You lived, for some of the time when you were small, with my father.

Who passed him on to me every time you passed him on to him, Iris says. Because he hadn't the first idea how to look after a small child.

I think he brought *us* up pretty well, his mother says.

Our mother brought us up, Iris says. Our father came home at 5.45pm and ate his supper.

He made the money that bought the suppers, his mother says.

Maybe he did. But he hadn't a clue what to do with a small child, Iris says. And your attempt to write me out of your son's history will fail. Because I'm safely locked in his memory bank whether he remembers it or not. And a memory bank is much less volatile and much more material than any of your contemporary financial institutions or hedge funds. Do you remember, Artie, the time I took you on the protest where we all did the dance holding up the big letters of the alphabet?

Art opens his eyes.

Yes! he says. I do remember something like that. I was the letter A.

You were the A in CASH NOT CUTS, Iris says.

Was I? Art says.

Then we did some footwork, some choreography, and you became the A in NO POLL TAX, Iris says.

He never lived with you. You never lived with her, his mother says.

Ah, we're a lucky generation, Philo, to have had all those angry summers, all that strength of feeling, the summers of such love, Iris says.

True, his mother says.

But their generation, Iris says. Summer of Scrooge. *And* the winter of Scrooge, *and* the spring, *and* the autumn.

Sadly also true, his mother says.

We knew not to want a world with war in it, Iris says.

We worked for something else, his mother says.

We were ourselves the vanguard, Iris says. We pitted our own bodies against the machines.

We knew our hearts were made of other stuff, his mother says.

Then a curious thing happens. His mother and his aunt start to sing. They fall together naturally into a song in another language. They sing it sweetly together at first, for the first couple of lines, then they break into harmony. His mother sings low and his aunt sings it high and they know it, how it falls and where to take it, as if they've rehearsed. They swing in and out of what sounds

like German into English then back into the other
language again.

It was always you from the start, they sing.

They sing it in their harmony, back to the
other language again, then the end of the song in
English.

You'd swear they were related, these two,
Lux says.

Yeah, and it's to me, Art says, God help me.

His mother and her sister sit in the same room
looking away from each other again. They're both
flushed. They both look triumphant.

I told him that story, not you, his mother says.

I told him it too, Iris says.

It will be a bit uncanny still to be thinking about
winter in April, say, and in such a balmy April with
the birds and the blossom, the leaves on their way,
and on such a sunny day, hottest day of the year so
far and a near-record high for the month.

But Art will be sitting on a train in all that
unexpected warmth and what he'll be seeing in his
head is the image of an old computer keyboard left
out in the snow, the flakes piling into each other
over it, soft, air-pocketed, settling above its letters
and numbers and symbols in a haphazard natural
architecture, and what he'll be thinking is:

how could she *know* to make a joke as complex
as *I refute it bus.*

How could she know more about his own culture than he did, and such interesting things, and not just know them but know them so well that she could make *jokes*, make jokes about a culture that isn't her culture and in a language that isn't her first language?

He will already have looked up online and read about Dr Samuel Johnson and the argument he had with the bishop about mind, matter, the structure of reality.

He will have passed repeatedly the fast food places called Chicken Cottage, seen pieces of Chicken Cottage advertising repeatedly stuck to pavements by rain and repeatedly known that mind and matter are mysterious and, when they come together, bounteous.

Come on, he'll have said to himself. Snap out of it. One flown bird doesn't stop the whole kingdom of birds from singing. It's just one gone bird.

Then he'll wonder if he's being a bit sexist thinking of a girl, a woman, in terms of birdlife.

But there *was* a bird, a rare bird, involved, and one he never got to see.

Which is why he's thinking it, he'll tell himself.

Plenty more birds in the sea, the man said.

Plenty more plastic bottles.

He'll remember the morning he paid her her salary in Cornwall, the £1,000 cash for the three days of being Charlotte.

She counted it, split it into different bundles and folded it into different pockets in her coat and jeans.

Thank you, she said.

Then he held out both his hands, inside one a five pound note and three pound coins, inside the other three unstruck matches.

She touched the hand with the money. She smiled.

You're a classy employer, guv, she said. I'd work for you again any day.

She touched the hand with the matches. She smiled again.

And a very classy man, she said.

She sat on the bedstuff and put the first of her studs back in, then the rings, then the little chain, then the silver bars. While she did, while she probed with the silver the inner tunnel of each hole in her skin (with a gentleness that gave him an erection then and still gives him one when he thinks about it months later), she looked round the barn at the Make Do stock, bits and pieces of it still unpacked on top of the crates after the people buying the things the day before.

We don't own things, she said. Look at them all looking back at us. We think they're ours, we can buy them, have them, throw them away when we're done with them. They know without having to know anything that it's us that are the throwaways.

My mother says you're really a good salesperson, he said.

I am, she said. It's one of my many skills.

Then she put her jacket on, kissed him and his mother on the cheek goodbye, got into Iris's car for the lift to the station for the early train and she left.

He waved. His mother waved. They waved from the door.

He went back into the barn full of all its stupid stuff, his chest feeling far too small.

By the side of the bedding she'd left a plastic water bottle, half full. He sat on the bedding and drank what was in it. *Still Scottish Mountain Water drawn from a sustainable source on the protected Glorat Estate in the heart of Scotland.*

Unruined water.

He wrapped the empty bottle inside his jumper and put it in his rucksack.

When he got back to the flat and unpacked it he put the bottle on the bedside table by the iPod dock, his Art in Nature notebooks, the phone charger.

One day in the spring to come, he'll sit on the bed and flick through an old notebook. He'll see in his handwriting the words *blatant* and *revealing*.

He'll have no idea why he ever wrote them down but he'll remember writing them on his hand in the Ideas Store.

He'll go, some weeks later, to the place Lux said she worked. Aw, Lux, they'll say. They'll call to each other. *A guy here's asking about Lux.* They'll tell him she got laid off in February, that ten people did and that she was one of them.

As he's leaving the place he'll see a few of the polystyrene packing things she told him about blowing round the yard in among what's left of last year's leaves.

He'll bend and pick one up.

!

It is so very light.

Then he'll go into the Ideas Store. It'll be the same woman on the main desk. He'll ask the woman about her, if she knows where she might be.

The woman won't recognize the name Lux.

He'll say, after he says the words piercings, thin, beautiful, witty, the phrase *one of the most intelligent people I've met, emotionally and intellectually.*

Oh, the librarian will say.

The librarian will explain how she had to eject the woman he's talking about from the library, but it was last year, quite some time ago.

She tried to sleep in here overnight, the librarian will say. I think she may well actually have managed it a few times. Without them knowing. I mean us knowing. It's strictly forbidden, I was in trouble enough with health and safety when she did, plus the rest of this building not being public any more, the rest being private property, it leaves the council open to lawsuits. I was instructed to ban her from the building. I couldn't do anything else and keep my job. How is she, do you know? This isn't a place to sleep, except, well, during the day obviously people fall asleep if they're tired and if there's no demand for the seat or whatever, well. Overnight though it's the fire risk and security issue. I couldn't. We can't.

The librarian will lean forward then and say more quietly:

if you see her, will you give her my love? Tell her Maureen at Ideas Store sends her love.

Boxing Day night. Art and Lux are wrapped in the bedding on the warm floor of the barn.

Lux is lying next to him with her head on his shoulder.

Nothing's happened, or happening, no sex or love or anything. His erection's all just a happy part of it. Lux is in his arms and he is in hers and because of this it's simple: Art's in heaven.

No, even better than heaven. Right now Art will never die. Art will live forever because her head is on his shoulder.

He tries to look down at her face. He can see from this angle the top of her head where her hair parting forms a curved road across it, then the suggestion of her eyelashes, her nose, part of her shoulder in her yellow T-shirt.

She is explaining to him how it is that she can be from somewhere else, and have been brought up somewhere else again, but still sound so like she grew up here.

It takes hard work, she says. Real graft and subtlety. It's a full-on education being from somewhere else in your country right now.

And can I ask you, he says. I'm not being rude. But for someone who lives from place to place, sometimes doesn't know where she'll sleep. You're so –

What? she says.

Clean, he says.

Ah, she says. That too takes real graft and subtlety.

She tells him his mother's got a tumble dryer out in the lobby by the back door. What does he think she's been doing in the middle of the night every night?

Then she tells him that she decided she'd talk to him at all, at the bus stop, in the first place, because she liked the cleanness of his own spirit.

I have a spirit? he says. A *clean* spirit?

Everything living has a spirit, she says. Without spirit we're nothing but meat.

And things like, say, flies and bluebottles, he says. Do they have spirits? Cause if I've got a spirit, I'm telling you. It's not clean, it's tiny, and rotten, and it's about the size of a bluebottle's.

The size of a bluebottle's spirit, she says. Shining in its armour. Have you ever seen a bluebottle's determination to get through the glass of a window?

I think you could maybe talk about anything, he says. There's nothing you wouldn't make interesting. Even I'm interesting when you talk about me.

She tells him she also decided she'd talk to him that day in the bus shelter because it was as if he was bracing himself against everything he touched and everything that touched him.

So I thought to myself, she says, I wonder what'll happen if he braces himself against me. Or me against him.

I'd bend. I'm a pushover. I'm like him, Art says nodding to the cardboard cut-out figure of Godfrey by the door.

You met him very little. Your theatrical father, she says.

I met him twice in all, he says. When I was very little myself. I told you, they were estranged. They were friends, but, well. He wasn't a part of my life.

He shrugs.

Once, after a show he was in, we all went for supper. I remember it vividly, I was eight. There were dancing girls from the chorus, the show was at a theatre in Wimbledon, Cinderella, he was one of the ugly sisters. It was exciting, the girls kept sitting me on their knees and making a great fuss of me is what I remember. I remember it more than I remember him. And the other time, we had our photos taken by a newspaper doing a piece on him, we had to pose round a Christmas tree holding presents. I don't remember doing it but we have the newspaper cutting somewhere. If I think of it I remember the cutting instead of what actually happened.

So I think of him, and I think of the word father, and it's kind of like there's a cut-out empty space in my head. I quite like it. I can fill it any way I like. I can leave it empty.

Though there are days when it's a bit like when they say a car cuts out, just stops, like all my ignition's gone.

But I like his style, Godfrey Gable. I like to think I've inherited it. Dignity regardless of what rubbish you're thinking about me. My favourite thing he did was an ad campaign for Branston's. We've got the publicity shots somewhere in all his stuff, it'll be in here somewhere in one of these boxes. He's holding a jar and looking at the camera with this witty look, and written next to his head it says:

I'm less a man who'll relish a challenge, more a man who'll challenge a relish.

I don't get it, Lux says.

Ah, he says. Quite hard to explain.

What's Branston's? she says.

They make pickle, he says. I'll find you when we're back in London and bring you a jar of it and we'll have it on cheese on toast.

Okay, she says. Depending what it tastes like. And since we're here, and since he's here with us, your cardboard father. Far be it from me to add to your rucksack when it comes to family matter. And not all the truths in our lives always get through the tight closed fists they're held in. But I think, one day, it'd be a good idea. You should talk with your mother, about your father.

Whatever, Art says.

And talking of your mother –, she says.

She sits up.

What time is it? she says. I've a date. We eat in the evenings, she and I. And I've got to wash and dry a couple of things.

She rolls herself out of the bedding. She pulls one of her boots on.

If I were you, she says, I'd stay here in the house with her a bit longer, till the start of the year maybe, and do like I've been doing. Get up and cook something in the middle of the night. She'll come down and eat with you if you do.

She'd never do that, he says. She'd send me away.

Lux pulls her other boot on.

Just talk with her, she says. Talk to her.

Nothing in common, he says.

Everything in common, Lux says. She's your

history. That's the other difference between meat and humans. I don't mean between animals and humans. They know how to evolve. We're more gifted than them, the chance to know where we came from. To forget it, to forget what made us, where it might take us, it's like, I don't know. Forgetting your own head.

She stands up.

I am even persuading myself, she says.

He shakes his head.

I can't do anything for her, he says. How can I? I'm family.

Try, she says.

No, he says.

You might as well try, she says.

No, he says.

You might, she says. I mean, given our histories. We both might.

Something a bit higher than his penis, something up in his chest, lifts.

Ha. Is that it, his spirit?

Might we? he says.

Close your eyes and open them.

It's high summer now.

Art is crossing a sombre London. There is a burnt-out building at the heart of the city.

It looks like a terrible mirage, a hallucination.

But it's real.

The building has gone up in flames so fast in the first place because it's been shoddily renovated, not being for the use or the residence of people with a lot of money.

Many people died.

There will be an argument happening all across politics and the media about how many people died because nobody can say for sure how many people were in the building that night, it being a place where a lot of people under the radar have been living.

Radar, Art thinks. World War Two invention for flushing out invisible enemies.

Standing on the tube in the heat he chances to read in a paper over someone's shoulder a piece of writing about how people are crowdfunding, raising thousands of pounds, to fund a boat that intercepts and waylays the rescue boats sent out from the Italian mainland to help the migrants in trouble in the sea.

He reads what he's just read again, to make sure he hasn't misread it.

Natural?

Unnatural?

He feels sick to his stomach.

As he reads the article for the third time, about people paying money to scupper other people's safety, the coastline swings into the tube train carriage, just a fragment of a second of it.

It juts across the top of everyone in the carriage.

He gets off the tube.

He walks past the British Library and he sees an image of Shakespeare outside it on a poster.

That's why Lux chose to live here, here of all the places on the earth.

They're bound to have a Shakespeare he can look at in their shop.

He goes in and crosses the courtyard. He stands in the security queue. He gets searched. He is really surprised by how bright it is in here, and how friendly, how open, how gracious. He sees the reception desk ahead of him. He sees the people in the cafe, the people sitting reading on a metal bench like a sculpture of a giant opened book. The book-bench has a large metal ball and chain attached to it, as if an integral part of it. Instead of going to the shop he surprises himself by going straight up to the desk and asking the woman behind the counter about why there's a ball and chain on that book-shaped bench. Is it so no one will steal the bench?

She tells him it's to signify that you mustn't steal a library book. In libraries in the old days, books used to be chained to their shelves, she says, so that they couldn't be taken away by any one individual, so that they'd always be there for everyone's use.

He thanks her. He asks her if it might be possible to speak, just for a moment, to the Library's Shakespeare expert.

She doesn't ask who or why. She doesn't say he'll need to make an appointment. She doesn't ask him for anything like proof of membership, anything at all. She picks up her phone's receiver and dials an extension number. Whom shall I say is calling? she says as she presses the buttons, and it isn't an old or fusty or bespectacled tweedy man who comes to the desk to meet Art. It's a young bright woman, the same age, younger than him maybe.

Oh, we don't have that here, she says when he explains. That's not part of our collection. But I know the folio you're describing. It's almost completely authentic, a real beauty. It's really something. The print of that flower runs across two late pages in Cymbeline.

Cymbeline, he says. The one about poison, mess, bitterness, then the balance coming back. The lies revealed. The losses compensated.

She smiles.

Beautifully put, she says. And the folio you're talking about with the print of the rose in it is in the Fisher Library in Toronto.

He sees, in her face, his own face fall and her see it happen.

Our own Shakespeare collection's pretty interesting too, even though I can't do you a pressed rose, she says.

He thanks her. He goes to the Library shop to see if they've got a Cymbeline. There's a Penguin

one on the Shakespeare shelves. On the cover it's
got a man from the past stepping out of a trunk
or a box.

He opens it at random. *Embraced by a piece of
tender air.* Oh, that's good.

His phone buzzes. It's a text from Iris in Greece.

*Dear Neph meant 2 tll u bfor I left yr mother has
movd hrslf into kitchn of house and all other rms
full of nothin but moths n spiders like in grt
xpctations x Ire.*

It's followed almost immediately by one from his
mother in Cornwall.

*Dear Arthur please ask your aunt to refrain from
reading and commenting on my private mail from
you; it is gross invasion of not just my privacy but
also yours. Also please ask her to confirm when she
is planning to return to Cornwall to stay because I
must sort my late summer diary and can plan no
movement of my own while your aunt is abroad
saving the world (again) and remaining
unforthcoming about her date of return.*

He's got into the habit of thinking up something
conceptual or metaphysical to ask them both every
week or so. He copies them both into everything he
sends them. This infuriates them. Good. They're of
the generation to enjoy infuriation, and the fury
keeps them in touch with one another as well as
with him. It's difficult sometimes, though, to think
what to ask them. So sometimes he asks them

something he imagines someone else might be likely to ask. He thought up a good Charlotte-like question last week.

Hi, it's me, your son and nephew. I have a question for you. What's the difference between politics and art?

His mother replied just to him: *Dear Arthur, Politics and Art are polar opposites. As a very fine poet once said, we hate poetry that has a palpable design upon us.* That'd be John Keats; his mother has read everything John Keats ever wrote and has even gone to Italy especially to see his grave. Such a narrow grassy space to hold such force of spirit, she said when she came back.

He copied this message to Iris.

Iris replied saying Keats was an anomaly, no Eton or Harrow or Oxbridge for him and that therefore every word Keats wrote and managed to publish was bloody well politicized all right *& th diff dear Neph is more betwn artist and politician – endlss enemies coz they both knw THE HUMAN will alwys srface in art no mtter its politics, & THE HUMAN wll hv t be absent or repressed in mst politics no mtter its art x Ire.*

He copied this to his mother. His mother replied just to him: *Dear Arthur, please stop sharing my private messages with your aunt, and dear Iris, since I know he'll copy this one to you too do you by any chance have a return date yet?*

The human will always surface.

Today when he gets home he sits outside his own front door at the top of the stairs behind the firedoors and composes a question he'd like, himself, to be able to ask Lux.

He knows that whatever she'd give as an answer would be enlightening.

Hi, it's me, your son and nephew. Why is it, what is it in us, in our natures, that means that people would want to pay actual money to make it difficult for other people not just to live but to be literally saved from dying?

He sends it with a link to the article he read over the person's shoulder on the tube. Then he goes in, sits on his bed and texts Charlotte the tender air quote in case it's useful for an Art in Nature.

Art in Nature is now a co-written blog by a communal group of writers.

(He's been asked to help write July.)

He surfs for a bit.

He reads, on the same site as the story about the people paying money to hurt people in the Mediterranean, an article about how a department store chain is about to start selling a teaset which reports back to the company that sells it via an app about how it weathers in the houses of the people who buy it or own it, what gets broken when, what gets most used, and what gets left in the box or the cupboard.

It reminds him of her again.

Lux.

How can anyone disappear so completely in such an age of everything tracked and known?

That's when he looks up online the library the woman in the British Library told him about, in Canada.

Fissure?

Fisher.

He checks through online images for an image. It's quite hard to find anything but eventually he does.

At least, he thinks he does. He looks at the photograph of an old page on his screen.

Is that it? Is that the flower?

That sort of smudgy mark?

The ghost of a flower is more what it looks like.

Who knows who pressed it in the book, who knows when? There it is.

The shape left by the bud makes it like the ghost of a flame too, like the shadow of a steady little flame.

He magnifies it on the laptop screen so he can see it more clearly.

He looks at it as closely as he can.

It's the ghost of a flower not yet open on its stem, the real thing long gone, but look, still there, the mark of the life of it reaching across the words on the page for all the world like a footpath that leads to the lit tip of a candle.

July:

it is a balmy day at the start of the month. An American President is making a speech in Washington at a rally to celebrate war veterans. The rally is called the Celebrate Freedom Rally.

The people in the crowd behind him and in front of him wave flags and chant the initials of the name of the country on earth that they live in.

Benjamin Franklin reminded his colleagues at the Constitutional Convention to begin by bowing their heads in prayer, he says. *I remind you that we're going to start saying Merry Christmas again.*

Then he talks about the words that are written on American money as if it's money itself that's the prayer.

Now it's a balmy day near the end of the month. The same American President is encouraging the

Scouts of America, gathered at the 2017 National Scout Jamboree in West Virginia, to boo the last President and to boo the name of his own opponent in last year's election.

And by the way, under the Trump administration, he says, *you'll be saying Merry Christmas again when you go shopping, believe me. Merry Christmas. They've been downplaying that little beautiful phrase. You're going to be saying Merry Christmas again, folks.*

In the middle of summer it's winter. White Christmas. God help us, every one.

Art in nature.

A number of books and resources about Greenham Common and twentieth century UK protest have helped in the writing of this book, especially texts by Caroline Blackwood and Ann Pettitt. A core inspiration was Elizabeth Sigmund's Rage Against the Dying (1980).

Huge thank you to Sophie Bowness and the Estate of Barbara Hepworth, and to Eleanor Clayton.

Thank you, Andrew and Tracy, and everybody at Wylie's.

Thank you, Simon.
Thank you, Lesley.
Thank you, Caroline, Sarah, Hermione, Ellie, Anna, and everyone at Hamish Hamilton.

Thank you, Kate Thomson.
Thank you, Lucy H.
Thank you, Mary.
Thank you, Xandra.

Thank you, Sarah.